Goodness and Mercy

Other Books by Debbie Viguié

The Kiss Trilogy

Kiss of Night
Kiss of Death
Kiss of Revenge

Sweet Seasons

The Summer of Cotton Candy
The Fall of Candy Corn
The Winter of Candy Canes
The Spring of Candy Apples
The Summer of Rice Candy

Witch Hunt

The Thirteenth Sacrifice
The Last Grave
The Circle of Blood

Goodness and Mercy

Psalm 23 Mysteries

By Debbie Viguié

Published by Big Pink Bow

Goodness and Mercy

ISBN-13: 978-1-7334281-4-9

Published by Big Pink Bow

www.bigpinkbow.com

To Jessica Sigman and Sarah Deeg.
Thank you both for your friendship and all the love and support you have given me. You’re my kind of crazy!

As always thank you to my husband, Scott, without whom none of this would be possible. Thank you also to my amazing parents, Rick and Barbara Reynolds. Thank you to the long-suffering Calliope Collacott for all her help and support. I would also like to thank all of the fans who have come along on this wild journey with me. The best is yet to come!

1

Rabbi Jeremiah Silverman had always loved Saturdays. He had loved them as a boy growing up in Israel. He had loved them even when he was an assassin for the Mossad. To a Jew it was a sacred day, a day of rest. Many viewed it as a complicated set of rules of what you could and could not do on the Sabbath, but he saw it for what it was meant to be. It was a respite from work, toil, the cares of the world, and ordinary life. It was a time of rejuvenation, reflection, worship, and joy. It was the mini vacation that he was able to take every week.

Well, except for this week.

Geanie was in front of him, blood trickling down her face from a cut above her eye where he'd hit her. She screamed and kicked him in the groin as hard as she could. He grunted as he dropped onto his knees. She screamed again as she drove her fingers into his throat hard enough to dislodge his Adam's apple. He fell backward as she sprinted away from him. At the edge of his vision, she slowed and turned.

"Did I kill you?" she screamed, her voice filled with fury.

He nodded.

"Good!"

Jeremiah lay there for a moment, struggling to catch his breath. He knew that Cindy, Joseph, Traci, and Mark were standing twenty feet away, watching. Today was going to be a day of reckoning. Their very lives could depend on what happened in the next hour.

He stood slowly to his feet. The body armor he was wearing shielded him from the majority of the impact of Geanie's blows. He was especially grateful for the collar that had kept her from actually dislodging his Adam's apple and killing him when she hit him in the throat.

Geanie moved to join the others who all wore looks of horror of varying degrees. Joseph busied himself wiping the blood off Geanie's face. The rest of her face was pale, almost translucent, and the blood stood out in sharp contrast.

Jeremiah looked at each one of them in turn.

Everyone had been in a state of alert since Mark's New Year's Eve phone call from the cult leader that was the father of Not Paul, Mark's dead partner. For four weeks Jeremiah had been teaching his friends self-defense. Initially, he had only planned to teach Cindy, but in light of everything that had happened in the past year and the phone call with its ominous warning, he had decided it was best to teach all his friends.

Mark had struggled the most as he had to break some of the training he'd had as a police officer. What Jeremiah was teaching him was not exactly standard operating procedure for officers. Well, at least not in America. All of Mark's training had focused on trying to subdue the subject. Jeremiah was focused on teaching him how to strike in order to kill an opponent or at least incapacitate them long enough to get away.

While Cindy had been his most eager student, Geanie had turned out to be the best. She was aggressive and did not hesitate to strike when he told her to. If anything, she had a problem dialing it back while sparring with the others. That was why she was only allowed to spar with him. That left Cindy and Mark to spar together and Joseph and Traci to spar together. It was definitely better that way with spouses not going against each other. It created too much of a difficult dynamic otherwise.

Today was the last official day of training, the culmination of all they'd learned. It was all about mastering just a small handful of highly effective moves. He wasn't training them to be fighters. He was training them to be survivors.

"Traci, step forward," Jeremiah said.

She did as he instructed. She was dressed in loose black slacks and a short sleeve shirt despite the coldness of the winter wind that was buffeting them. Her hair was pulled back in a tight braid. He stared into her eyes and she stared back, unflinching.

"We are not friends. There are no friends here," he said, his voice a low growl. "Do you understand me?"

"Yes," she said, softly but firmly.

"I will not hold back. Do you understand?"

"Yes," she said, raising her chin slightly.

"I am going to kill you unless you stop me."

He didn't wait for her to acknowledge what he said. He lunged toward her. He did not attack her in the same way as he had attacked Geanie. That wouldn't be a fair test since she would subconsciously be expecting that. Instead, he swept her legs out from under her and dropped her to the ground. He wrapped his hand around her throat and began to squeeze.

He could see the fear and panic in Traci's eyes, and he silently willed her to fight back. He wouldn't give her quarter, though. He would keep squeezing until she lost consciousness if he had to. She and the others had to know what it would be like, how they would feel and react, if someone was trying to kill them. He saw in her eyes the moment desperation struck. In that moment he was no longer her trusted friend but the man who was trying to kill her. She drove her thumbs up swiftly, jabbing at his eyes. She moved so quickly he barely was able to jerk his head backward in time. She took advantage of his movement and rolled away, breaking his hold on her. She was up on her feet and running before he could react. Unlike Geanie she hadn't delivered a decisive blow, but she had achieved the ultimate goal—escape.

Jeremiah stood up, nodding his approval. In the end she had done what she needed to do even if it had taken her longer than Geanie to respond. Ideally, he would have brought in another instructor, a stranger, for the testing. It would have made it easier for his friends to strike out and try to hurt him. They didn't have that luxury, though, and this did teach them a very valuable lesson. Sometimes danger came from the most unexpected source. Just because you knew someone didn't mean they wouldn't try and kill you.

"Traci, come back!" he shouted.

She stopped running and made her way slowly back to the group. When she got close he could see that there was already bruising around her throat. Mark saw it, too, and he turned to glare at Jeremiah.

"How could you hurt her?" Mark demanded.

Logically the detective knew why, but he wasn't being logical. He was being a husband.

Jeremiah shook his head. "I'd do it again a dozen times if it saved her life one day."

Mark actually snarled at him and for a moment Jeremiah was convinced the other man was going to rush him. He hadn't planned on dealing with Mark next, but this would end up being an even better test since his friend's emotions were so heightened. Above all else Mark needed to learn when to attack and when to retreat. He didn't do either of those very well. To that end Jeremiah decided to bait him.

"After all, she can't rely on you to protect her since you've done such a terrible job of that the last few years," Jeremiah said. "I mean, she'd be better off completely alone than ever looking to you for anything."

Mark leaped forward with a roar and Jeremiah punched him in the nose.

~

Cindy stared in fascinated horror as Mark circled Jeremiah. Traci came up next to her and started screaming for Mark to kill Jeremiah. It was completely disconcerting and Cindy dearly wanted to shout for Jeremiah. She realized, though, that in order for the weeks of training to mean anything that Mark had to win. At least, Mark had to successfully execute a couple of the moves Jeremiah had taught them.

She glanced around at the others. Joseph was still busy treating the cut on Geanie's head, concern wrinkling his brow. Truth be told, she was worried about them. The last few weeks had been hard on everyone, but the stress was showing for both of them. Joseph was more quiet than usual, and she often caught him frowning. When she asked what was wrong, though, he'd just smile and tell her it was nothing.

He was lying, of course. She just didn't know what about.

Meanwhile Geanie had been edgy and super aggressive with the training, almost frighteningly so. Cindy wasn't sure if there was something else going on or if Geanie's natural exuberance was causing her to attack training with gusto. She'd been glad after their first sparring session that Jeremiah had decided to have Geanie just spar with him. She'd sworn at one point that Geanie was actually going to try to hurt her. She'd been completely focused on the technique to the point of ignoring the person on the receiving end.

Cindy figured that was a good thing because it meant Geanie was ready to take on an actual assailant.

Unlike me, she thought in frustration.

She had honestly believed that given everything she had been through that she would have been more aggressive, more excited to actually learn the moves to defend herself and disable an attacker. She hadn't been able to forget, though, that it was friends she was going up against. She only hoped that she'd learned and internalized enough that it would be useful in an actual emergency.

Jeremiah hit Mark hard enough to send the other man staggering back. Cindy winced. That was going to leave some bruising.

Come on, Mark, she thought. Just remember what he's taught you.

Next to her Traci was still shouting so loudly that Cindy almost didn't hear her phone ring. Once she did, though, she decided to ignore it. She would call whoever it was back after the training session.

Jeremiah cocked his head to the side, simultaneously avoiding a punch from Mark.

"Cindy, answer your phone," he said, his voice a bit off.

It startled her, but after a moment of staring at him she hurried over to her purse and fished around in it for her phone.

She saw that the call was from St. Joseph's. Heart in her throat, she answered it.

"Hello, this is Cindy," she said.

"Hello, Cindy. We've talked before. This is Dr. Tripp from St. Joseph's Hospital in New Orleans."

"Yes, I remember," she said, startled.

St. Joseph's Hospital was where Dr. Gerald Wilson, the writer who had interviewed her about her part in the Passion Week Killer events, was in a coma. He'd been that way for almost two years. The last thing he'd done was try to warn Cindy that a notorious cult leader was still alive.

"How is Dr. Wilson?" she asked, feeling guilty that in all the craziness it had been a few months since she had called to check. She'd called every week for the first two months, then less and less. At some point it had started to seem like he would never wake up.

"He's in the ICU right now."

"Why, what happened?" she asked.

"Last night he woke up."

"He did? That's great!" Relief flooded through her, but a moment later she processed the rest of what he'd said. "Wait, why is he in the ICU?"

"An hour after he woke up, someone tried to kill him."

2

"It involves all of us," Geanie said heatedly.

Mark disagreed completely. Geanie and Joseph were, at the last, only tangentially involved. There was no reason for them to risk their lives on this. Same with Traci. She needed to stay here where it was safe.

Of course, she wasn't exactly safe. None of them were since the threatening call at New Year's. He could feel anger roiling in his stomach. It helped to counter the fear that was making him sweat.

They were gathered in Joseph and Geanie's kitchen, following the revelation that Gerald was awake and had been attacked. The phone call had ultimately cut their training session short. In his estimation that was a good thing since he'd been unsuccessful in his attempts to disable Jeremiah.

The revelation that Dr. Wilson was awake and that he'd been attacked within minutes of waking had first excited then angered him. Mark felt certain that the same man who had put Gerald in the coma was the one who had come after him once he was out. The only question was, how did he know?

Mark was convinced that someone who worked at the hospital must have fed the monster the information, either deliberately or unintentionally. After all, it wouldn't have been that hard for Matthews to get himself put on a call list to be notified if Gerald woke up.

Of course, Mark couldn't be certain of anything while he was sitting in a mansion in California, more than halfway across the country. He needed to be there to help guard Gerald and to track down his assailant. He couldn't do either of those, though, if he was worried about his loved ones getting hurt. That was why he had proposed that he travel to New Orleans alone.

He had known there would be objections to his plan. He just hadn't realized they would be so vehement, especially from Traci.

"I'm not letting you go by yourself," Traci said.

"Fine, I'll take Jeremiah with me," Mark said.

"And you're crazy if you think you're both going without me," Cindy said pertly.

"Okay, the three of us," he said, knowing from experience that it was not possible to separate Cindy and Jeremiah when one of them thought the other was in danger.

"We're all going," Geanie said firmly after sharing a quick look with Joseph.

"That seems like overkill," Mark said.

"Oh no, bad things happen when the six of us split up," Joseph said, clearly taking his wife's side.

"You mean worse than the things that happen when we're all together?" Mark asked sarcastically.

"Hawaii," Geanie said.

"That was pretty bad," Cindy murmured, blanching slightly.

"Las Vegas," Joseph said.

"Also bad," Cindy said.

"Israel," Geanie said.

"Not much is worse than that," Jeremiah admitted.

"Cattle drive," Joseph said.

"Worse," Mark and Jeremiah said in unison.

"So, it's settled. We're all going," Joseph said with an air of finality. "We can celebrate Mardi Gras and Valentine's while we're at it."

"How long do you think we're going to be gone?" Mark asked.

Joseph shrugged. "As long as we need to be to get things taken care of."

"Amen," Traci said fervently.

Mark was outvoted and he knew it. He turned to Jeremiah, hoping the other man might have something persuasive to say on the topic. He only shrugged.

"I guess we're going to New Orleans," Mark grumbled.

"Perfect!" Traci said brightly. "The twins and Buster can stay with my sister."

He couldn't believe how excited Traci looked. Just a few weeks before she'd been a nervous wreck. He'd been worried that she was heading for a complete breakdown. The training with Jeremiah seemed to have helped, though. Maybe it had given her some small sense of control or empowerment. Maybe it had just been therapeutic for her to be able to hit someone. Joseph still bore some slight bruising from a black eye she'd given him the week before while they were sparring. Fortunately, the other man had taken it in stride. He'd even joked about it, telling people he'd been beat up by a girl.

"I'll have to get the time off work," Mark said. He knew, in truth, it wouldn't be an issue. Things had been slow, and he had a lot of vacation time coming. Half the precinct would likely be glad he wasn't there. Some people never forget, he thought ruefully.

"I can ask Marie to look after Captain. You could leave Blackie at my house with him," Jeremiah said to Cindy.

"Actually, why don't we ask Liam and Rebecca to housesit and take care of them and Clarice?" Geanie suggested.

Mark raised an eyebrow as he imagined his partner and his girlfriend having the run of Joseph's mansion.

"You think he'd say yes?" Joseph asked.

"I think he'd do backflips," Mark said.

"And babysitting the fur babies will be good practice for them," Traci said with a knowing look. "After all, if they want to have kids some day…" she trailed off.

"Well, if you really want to put them through a trial by fire, you could leave Ryan and Rachel with them," Mark said with a straight face.

"Um, no," Traci answered. "I love Liam, but…"

She doesn't trust him completely, Mark thought in a rush. That was crazy, though. Liam had never given her any reason to doubt him. Maybe it was his girlfriend, then. They should probably spend some time getting to know her better. Or it could have something to do with the fact that my previous partner is the reason why we're all learning self-defense and heading off to New Orleans in the first place.

It was true. Paul, or Not Paul as they often called him, had left a mess behind when he died. Four years later they were still dealing with the aftermath and there were days it felt like they always would be. The ominous call on New Year's Eve from Not Paul's cult leader father was still giving Mark nightmares.

"So, when do we leave?" Cindy asked.

"Tomorrow," Joseph said firmly. "I don't think we can afford to leave Gerald alone longer than that."

Cindy nodded, looking relieved but also troubled.

"What's wrong?" Traci asked, also noticing the church secretary's expression.

"With both Geanie and I gone, it's going to cause some problems for the church. There's Sunday programs, the newsletter, and other things that we have to work on this week."

"I've already got that covered," Geanie said with a mysterious smile.

"Care to share with the rest of the class?" Mark asked.

"When we went back to work after New Year's I downloaded all the files and software we'd need to work remotely onto the laptop I got for Christmas. That way we can handle the church business even if we can't be there."

"That was my idea," Joseph said.

"And since we updated the phone system at the beginning of the year so that callers can directly access voicemail for who they want to speak to, the daily volunteers can handle the few phone calls that are general information," Geanie said, smirking. "And since all of our current volunteers have been at it for at least a couple of years, they're usually just as helpful with walk-ins as we could be."

"The new phone system was also my idea. I was the one who talked the committee into going for it," Joseph said. "It allows for greater efficiency for members without getting rid of the human touch for non-members."

"He was brilliant," Geanie said with obvious pride.

Mark knew that Cindy's frequent absenteeism had caused her problems with work almost a year earlier. Of course, it wasn't her fault that trouble, and dead bodies, seemed to gravitate her way. It looked like Geanie and Joseph had found a viable solution, though.

"You guys are the best," Cindy said with a grin.

I wonder if she's going to keep working at the church after she and Jeremiah get married? Mark had a strange feeling that her days at First Shepherd were numbered.

"Excuse me a moment," Joseph said, heading into the other room with his phone.

"This should be fun. I've always wanted to see New Orleans," Traci said.

"It's going to likely be upsetting and scary, too," Mark warned.

She shrugged and he wished he knew what was going on in her head.

~

Cindy had to hand it to Geanie and Joseph. When they made up their minds about something, they did so emphatically and executed their decision with style.

They were nearing the end of their flight to New Orleans. It was the first time she'd flown on Joseph's private jet, and it had been an eye-opening experience. She'd spent the entire flight sitting with her legs stretched out while chatting with her friends or walking around without bumping into anyone. The food had been sensational, too. The last few times she'd flown she'd been subjected to small, overpriced snack boxes.

This is how traveling was meant to be, she thought with a contented sigh as the pilot announced that they were going to be making their descent soon. She almost didn't want to land. New Orleans held danger and fear and potential death. Up here in the sky in the luxury plane it was as though all her cares were far away from her. It was like they had been left behind at the airport.

"I could totally get used to this," Traci said, voicing Cindy's own thoughts.

"I know, right?" Geanie said. "I'll be honest. I'm still not used to it."

"Then you're not doing it right," Traci said with a small laugh.

"You haven't told us where we're staying yet," Traci said. "The Ritz-Carlton, Windsor Court, The Roosevelt?"

"Nowhere so high profile," Joseph broke into the conversation. "I didn't want it to be that easy to find us."

"And traveling by private jet is so discreet," Cindy said, unable to stop from teasing.

"It is when our names are nowhere attached to the flight plans or even the ownership of the plane," Joseph said with a smile.

"I'm impressed," Cindy said.

"You should be," Joseph said with a smile. "Actually, anonymity is kind of a hobby for me."

Cindy looked at him closely and realized that with the kind of money Joseph had privacy probably was a primary concern. Sometimes she forgot that there were some benefits to being just a regular citizen. Of course, if she'd been a regular citizen, her name would have been all over the passenger lists for a commercial flight.

And my legs would be aching.

~

Twenty minutes later they had landed at the airport. A private car service had met them on the tarmac and whisked them toward their destination. It turned out they were staying at a small hotel just off Bourbon Street. The charm and ambience of the place with all its wrought iron balconies filled Cindy's heart with a kind of wonder and excitement.

New Orleans had been on her list of places that she wanted to see before she died. Her thoughts darkened only slightly when she reflected that she was here because she was trying to keep someone else from dying.

"This place is amazing!" Traci said. "It's like I always dreamed. I mean, when I think New Orleans, this is exactly what I think of," she said as they walked through a courtyard.

"Glad it meets with your approval," Joseph said as he returned from the front desk.

He handed out room keys along with city maps.

"We're all on the second floor in a row," he said. "We have four rooms."

Cindy nodded wistfully. In a few more months she and Jeremiah would be able to share a room. She glanced over at him and saw by the way he was staring at her that he was clearly thinking along the same lines. It made her blush.

"And these are for you," Joseph said, handing Jeremiah a small bundle.

"What are those?" Cindy asked.

"Duplicate keys to all our rooms," Joseph said. "You can never be too careful."

~

Jeremiah was grateful that Joseph had gotten him keys for all the rooms. It saved him the trouble of acquiring them. He wasn't happy that Cindy was going to be in a room by herself, but her room was situated between his and Mark and Traci's. If something happened, they both should hear it.

They made it to the second floor with their luggage. He let himself into his room. He noticed the quaintness of it, but almost as an afterthought. The balcony that overlooked the courtyard caught his attention. It made for a good vantage point to watch the comings and goings around the hotel. It also provided a secondary escape route. He would have to do a little extra work, though, to secure it as it was a soft entry point.

He put his luggage down and glanced at the extra keys. He took a marker from his bag and made marks on each so he could easily see at a glance which card key went to which room. His hand lingered on the key to Cindy's room.

~

Cindy turned on the light in her room and dropped her luggage just inside the doorway. She crossed the room and threw open the curtains to the balcony and marveled for a moment at the view into the courtyard below. It was beautiful and everything she had ever pictured when she thought of New Orleans.

Something was bothering her, though. She turned back and scanned the room. She slowly walked closer to the bed. Something didn't feel right. It looked like there was a mask on the pillow. Maybe it was a Mardi Gras thing the hotel did. There was a notecard beside it, standing open like a tent. She started to reach her hand down then froze. It wasn't a Mardi Gras mask that stared up at her with empty eyes. It was someone's face.

3

Somehow Jeremiah wasn't surprised when he heard Cindy scream. He was in motion before he even had a chance to think it through. He yanked the door open and ran into the hall, nearly colliding with Mark who had done the same.

Jeremiah slammed the keycard to Cindy's room against the lock and a moment later was inside. He quickly scanned the room before moving to her side. She was staring down at something on the bed.

"What's wrong?" Mark asked.

"It's human, right?" Cindy asked, voice shaking.

Jeremiah looked down. There on her pillow was a grotesque mask that did indeed look like it was made from human skin.

A killer took the skin off someone's face and dried it, he realized as he stared grimly at the token. It was impossible to tell age, gender, or even the race of the victim given the condition the skin mask was in.

"Oh my…" Mark trailed off. Jeremiah glanced at the detective who looked like he might be sick.

"Is everything okay?" Joseph asked from the doorway.

"Don't come in here. And don't let the girls in," Jeremiah said grimly.

He grabbed Cindy by the shoulders and pulled her away, moving her toward the door. He handed her off to Joseph who looked worried but didn't ask.

"Come with me," he murmured, leading her out of the room.

Jeremiah grabbed a tissue from the bathroom and walked back to the bed. He gingerly used it to pick up the card that was next to the mask.

"What does it say?" Mark asked quietly.

Jeremiah read out loud. "Welcome to my town. Enjoy Carnival. Let the festivities begin!"

"That is one sick… do you think it's Matthews?" Mark asked.

"What other enemies does Cindy, do any of us, have here?" Jeremiah asked.

He set the card back down exactly where it had been.

"Time to introduce ourselves to the local police," Mark said with a sigh. "The officer I spoke with when Gerald was first admitted to the hospital was a Detective Lorraine Lewis. We'll start there," Mark said, pulling out his phone.

~

Detective Lewis was on duty and managed to arrive at their hotel in less than twenty minutes.

Detective Lewis turned out to be not at all what Mark had expected. She was beautiful with dark skin, black, shoulder-length hair, and startlingly green eyes. Taking into account her looks, combined with her height which had to be close to six feet, one could be forgiven for thinking she was a model.

"Detective Walters, I presume," she said in soft tones as she smiled at him.

"Detective Lewis, sorry we're meeting under these circumstances," he said with an answering smile.

A short, squat man with a bulbous nose walked into the room moments later.

"This is my partner, Detective Ray Moretti," she said.

"How do you do?" Mark said.

Moretti nodded, but didn't say anything. His eyes, however, swept Mark from head to toe before he turned and gave the room a thorough once over. His eyes finally rested on Jeremiah who had been standing there quietly the entire time.

"This is Rabbi Jeremiah Silverman. His fiancée was the one who found the mask in question," Mark said.

Jeremiah inclined his head, but, like Moretti, stayed silent.

Lorraine smirked. "Well, Mark, may I suggest we get on with it while our laconic associates stand and stare at each other?" she asked.

"By all means," he said.

He pointed toward the mask and note on the bed. "Cindy Preston came in and found these waiting here for her. We had just checked into the hotel."

"Then how did you arrive at the conclusion that they were meant for her?" Lorraine asked as she moved over to the bed.

"Because I know Cindy," Mark said with a sigh.

Lorraine turned and looked at him quizzically.

He grimaced. "We're here because Dr. Gerald-"

"Woke up and was subsequently attacked. I'm aware," she said, interrupting.

"Yes, well, you're not the only one," Mark said. "Read the card."

She pulled a pair of gloves out of her jacket pocket and carefully put them on before picking up the card. She read it out loud and then glanced at her partner who nodded.

"Any enemies?" she asked.

"Presumably whoever attacked Gerald," Mark said.

Lorraine nodded. She glanced at Jeremiah who continued to stand, stoically watching her and her partner.

"Where is Miss Preston now?" Lorraine asked.

"With our other friends who traveled here with us," Mark said.

"I'll need to speak with all of them," Lorraine said.

"Of course," Mark said.

She turned her attention to the mask of human skin.

"A gruesome message. Someone does not like her," Lorraine said.

She held out her hand and her partner stepped forward, pulling a pair of tweezers from his pocket and handing them to her.

Lorraine carefully used the tweezers to pick up the mask and turn it over.

"Or maybe they like her a little too well," she said softly.

Mark stepped forward to see what it was Lorraine was looking at. There, on the other side of the mask, the killer had glued several small pictures of Cindy. Each of them looked to have been clipped from a newspaper.

Jeremiah took a step forward and Mark shook his head fiercely. The rabbi narrowed his eyes but stepped back again. Mark wasn't sure why he didn't want the other man seeing what he was looking at. Jeremiah was used to staying calm, and being unemotional in front of strangers.

Maybe too much so, Mark thought. Lorraine struck him as the type who didn't miss much. If Jeremiah kept too tight a check on his emotions under the circumstances it would stand out.

"Your initial assessment proves to be right," Lorraine said, turning to look at Mark. "Someone went to a lot of trouble to send Miss Preston a message."

~

Jeremiah wasn't sure why Mark had waved him off, but he trusted the other man enough to stand back despite the fact that curiosity was nearly eating him alive. Actually, it was more than curiosity. It was a burning need to know as much as possible about whoever had done this. He had carefully studied the mask while waiting for the police to arrive. There were no rips or tears in it. Whoever had removed the skin had known what they were doing and had been very careful, very precise in their efforts.

The strategy the two New Orleans detectives were using was highly effective and he had no doubt it had served them well throughout their partnership. With her beauty and charm Detective Lewis drew all eyes to her, freeing her partner up to observe and investigate without drawing attention or suspicion. Already the man had taken stock of everything and everyone in the room. At one point he did a slow turn in the room that went unnoticed by Mark.

Jeremiah had seen one man in his previous career who did such things. He had a photographic memory and was able to walk through the images later and pick out even the slightest detail he might have initially missed. It was a rare gift, but Jeremiah was certain it was one that Detective Moretti shared. He would need to take extra precautions when dealing with the man. They all would.

We are the victims here, Jeremiah reminded himself. To that end he let worry slide onto his face.

"What is it?" he asked, allowing his concern to show in his voice.

"Newspaper clippings, photos of Cindy, are glued on the inside," Mark said.

Rage and worry filled him and with great effort he was able to allow the latter to show without betraying the former.

"What kind of a monster would do this?" he asked.

"A very precise one," Detective Lewis said as she examined the mask more closely. "He didn't have as much time as he would have liked, though. Either that or he is not as creative as he thinks he is."

"How do you figure that?" Mark asked.

"He left this mask for Carnival. It's plain, unadorned on the outside. I would have painted it."

"That's dark," Mark blurted out.

Detective Lewis just shrugged. "This is New Orleans. Dark is a matter of opinion."

And in a flash Jeremiah understood her. He didn't know what her story was, but he knew that she'd been touched by darkness in some profound way.

~

Cindy was sitting in Geanie and Joseph's room telling them and Traci what she'd found. All three looked shaken and Joseph was downright angry.

"I picked this hotel because they're known for their discretion. This is where celebrities stay when they want to hide from the press. I made the reservation twenty-four hours ago and somehow a psychopath knew we were coming and was in our room before we even checked in. This never should have been able to happen. I paid a lot of money to ensure it wouldn't."

Cindy was surprised to discover that with everything they'd been through together, she'd never seen Joseph this rattled before.

"Money can't protect us from this guy," she muttered.

Somehow that seemed to just upset Joseph more. He began pacing the room like a caged tiger.

"Let's think this through. It's not possible that he's got the entire town wired," he said.

"Why not?" Traci asked.

He turned and looked at her. "Because to cover every hotel that takes a level of money and influence that's unthinkable."

"The government does things like that when there's a manhunt on," Traci pointed out.

"That's the government. They're doing it legally. There are mechanisms, channels for that," Joseph said. "This guy would have to have an in everywhere and that's just not possible."

"Unless he's using one of the government mechanisms," Traci said.

Joseph sat down heavily.

"That's a terrifying thought," he said.

Cindy agreed.

"Let's assume that neither is true," Geanie said. Her voice sounded calm, but her face was ashen.

"Then what does that leave us with?"

"Say, you're Matthews and you just failed to kill Gerald when he came out of his coma," Geanie said.

"I wouldn't have failed," Joseph growled darkly.

"Maybe he didn't."

"What do you mean?" Traci asked Geanie.

"What if he wasn't trying to kill him, but was just trying to make it look like he was?"

"Why would he do that?" Cindy asked.

They all turned to stare at her. Several seconds passed before it sunk in.

"You think he did it to lure us…me… here?" she asked.

"It worked, didn't it?" Geanie said quietly.

Cindy lurched to her feet, feeling the sudden need to get out of there. She headed for the door, but then stopped. Jeremiah and Mark were still dealing with the police. Besides, where would she go that she would know she'd be safe?

"So, he lured us here. How did he know we'd come to this hotel?" Joseph asked.

"I think you said it yourself," Traci said. "Everyone looking for anonymity comes here. A local would probably know that. If you knew that someone was coming to the city but didn't want to be seen, isn't this one of the first places you'd stake out? I mean this and private home rentals and you could hack the websites to handle those."

"He might not have even been thinking it through that much," Geanie said. "He knew we'd come in by plane. He could have easily guessed we'd hire a car service. There can't be that many. It wouldn't be as hard to hack a couple of companies' records or bribe someone at each company to keep a look out for us."

"You're right," Joseph said. "And when I booked the car, I told them where I was going. He had plenty of time to figure out what rooms we'd be in and to break into Cindy's room and leave that for her."

"I wonder what the note says," Geanie mused.

"We'll find out soon enough," Joseph said grimly. "As soon as Mark and Jeremiah are done talking to the police."

"The police will be ready to talk to us at that point," Traci said.

"We need to be careful what we tell them," Geanie pointed out.

"You're right," Joseph said. "They don't know us, and even if they did…"

A sudden, sick feeling was writhing in Cindy's stomach. It started the moment Geanie said they needed to be careful what they told the police. She was right, of course. It was worse than that, though.

They needed to be careful what they told their enemy.

"Everyone stop talking!" she barked.

They all turned again to look at her. Clearly wondering what was going through her mind.

She took a couple of deep breaths. She'd been through this before, but Jeremiah had been there to handle it and figure things out. She stood up and cast her gaze around the room.

It was foolish to think that Matthews had gone to all the trouble of finding them only to leave something in her room. He would have been in each of their rooms. Even if he didn't leave the others notes or masks made out of human faces he would have left something else.

He was almost certainly listening to every word they said.

4

Jeremiah's eyes kept moving around the room. So many thoughts were running through his mind. He figured that Matthews had probably learned where they were staying from the car company. The question was, how far in advance had he known? It would have taken quite a while to make the mask itself. Hopefully he'd focused all his time on that and there were no other surprises, like incendiary devices, hidden in Cindy's room or any of the others. Until the detectives left, he wouldn't be able to tell for sure.

Of course, he might not have time even then. He was certain that they wouldn't be staying at this hotel. As soon as the detectives were gone, they would be, too. This time he'd work with Joseph to find them more secure lodging and to get there without being detected. At least, that was the plan.

He didn't like that Matthews, or someone working for him, seemed to be able to strike so quickly. He or they were more organized than one would expect for a former cult leader who should have a vested interest in lying low. Then again, this was his hometown and who knew how deep his roots ran. There could be any number of people who owed him favors or allegiance of one kind or another. One thing was certain. They were deep in enemy territory and they'd have to tread very, very carefully.

Ray was staring intently at the back of the television set. After a moment the detective pulled a device into view. It was a crude listening device, its placement sloppy. Jeremiah watched as Ray showed it to Lorraine.

"Gentlemen, it would appear that we have an audience," Lorraine said, eyes narrowed.

Jeremiah noted that she didn't even bother to try and play it cool. Apparently, she was fine with the listener knowing that their bug had been discovered.

"Announce it, why don't you?" Mark said sarcastically.

Lorraine shrugged and studied the device. Jeremiah was able to see it well enough from where he was standing.

Not only was the device fairly basic but it had also been placed in a spot where it had been easy to locate. That seemed odd. Either it was a decoy and the real device was hidden somewhere else or it was put in hastily. Neither felt quite right to him, though.

It was entirely possible that the man they were after hadn't bothered to put something more sophisticated in, because he didn't expect them to stay past the police visit.

He expects us to change hotels. He knows we won't stay so he didn't bother putting in more effort.

It was so obvious that Jeremiah caught himself shaking his head. If it had just been him, he would have chosen to stay right there, if only to keep his adversary guessing. It wasn't just him, though. He was responsible for five other people, including the woman he loved. While it was likely that the man who had left the mask had simply picked the lock, Jeremiah couldn't rule out the possibility that he'd had help breaking into the room. Even if he didn't know anyone at the hotel, a disarming smile and a well-placed hundred-dollar bill could turn a lot of heads, particularly among some of the lower paid, much abused staff. Jeremiah himself had done something similar on a number of occasions when he wanted access to a room.

"What do you think?" Ray asked Lorraine.

She shook her head. "I think Miss Preston has herself a stalker."

~

Mark hated having to keep the other detectives at arm's length, but there were some things about his friends that were better left unexplained. When Lorraine and her partner finally went to Joseph and Geanie's room to question the others Mark was free to talk to Jeremiah.

Before he could say anything, though, the rabbi held a finger to his lips.

He doesn't want to say a word in case there's another listening device, Mark realized.

Mark started to look around, but quickly realized he was out of his depth. He stepped back and watched Jeremiah work. It was impressive. The rabbi was quick and thorough. He checked places that Mark would never even have thought of. He went so far as to flip over both of the chairs at the small table and check the seams on the undersides.

Jeremiah took out a pocketknife and used the knife to unscrew the cover to the air vent in the room. Mark's eyes nearly bugged out when Jeremiah pulled a small, cobweb-covered box out of the vent. It looked like it had been sitting untouched for years judging by the amount of dust piled up on it. Jeremiah set the box down on the table and gingerly opened it.

Inside was a handgun, a box of bullets, and some papers. Jeremiah rifled through them for a moment before replacing the lid and turning to put the box back into the wall.

"What are you doing?" Mark asked, breaking the silence.

"Putting it back," Jeremiah said.

"Why? That's a gun. We should turn it over to the police."

"And tell them what?" Jeremiah asked, a twinge of impatience in his voice. "I'm sure they'd love to hear why I decided to go looking for it and how I found it."

"But it could belong to a criminal or…"

"A spy? An assassin?" Jeremiah asked, a dusting of sarcasm in his voice.

"Something like that."

"Look, Mark. It's been here a long time. I'm guessing whoever put it here is in no position to come back for it. And if they are, then they might need it pretty badly."

As soon as Jeremiah had replaced the grate on the vent he turned back to Mark.

"The place is clean," he said.

"Is that a good thing?" Mark asked.

"Matthews or whoever is behind the mask was counting on the fact that we wouldn't be staying. He didn't bother putting in anything more elaborate."

"What about the other rooms?" Mark asked.

"I'm assuming we'll find it's the same, but we should check them just in case there are any more surprises."

"Let's do it now while the detectives are still talking to the others," Mark said. "That way when they're done, we'll all be ready to get the heck out of here."

"Agreed," Jeremiah said.

He picked up Cindy's bags and headed out the door. "Let's check your room first," he said.

~

Cindy was getting tired of the endless barrage of questions from the two New Orleans detectives. She was familiar enough with the police process to know that they were just being thorough, but it felt like they were losing precious time they needed to figure out what was going on before their enemy could attack Gerald again.

"Look, we need to go talk to Gerald and help stop this guy before he strikes again," Cindy finally said, unable to keep the exasperation out of her voice.

The horror over the skin mask had slowly been sublimated by her desire to get out of the hotel room and do something. It literally felt like there was an alarm clock ticking in her mind and she didn't know when it was going off but it felt like it would be soon.

"You seem quite confident that whoever attacked him was the selfsame person who violated the sanctity of your room," Lorraine said.

"Aren't you?" Cindy asked pointedly.

Before Lorraine could say anything, Jeremiah and Mark came into the already crowded room, lugging suitcases with them.

"What do we have here?" Lorraine asked, arching one perfect eyebrow while Ray skulked in the corner of the room.

"Our bags. We won't be staying at this establishment after all," Mark said, clearly struggling and failing to keep the sarcasm out of his voice.

"When we're finished here, we can drive you to another hotel," Ray said.

"No, thank you," Mark said. "We've made our own arrangements."

Cindy nodded, glad that he and Jeremiah had clearly had a chance to talk things out.

"You okay, darling?" Jeremiah asked as he put down her suitcase and came over to her.

"Fine, just getting really tired and very worried about Gerald."

~

It took another two hours, but the police finally cleared out and so did Cindy and her friends. Over the next couple of hours they walked, took two buses, an Uber, and 3 different taxis to arrive at their new location where they checked in under assumed names. A private word between Joseph and the manager was able to arrange it and they soon found themselves with two suites at The Roosevelt.

"I only registered two people for each room and had them separated so anyone looking for six people or a group of three or four rooms won't find us," Joseph said when they arrived upstairs at the first room which was across the hall from the second.

"How trustworthy is the manager?" Mark asked.

"He's the cousin of one of my friends from college. I think he'll be fine," Joseph said.

"Convenient," Traci muttered.

"It worked out for us," Joseph said with a shrug.

They all took seats in the living room area.

"So, what's next?" Geanie asked.

"I want to go to the hospital and see Gerald," Cindy said. "We need to let him know he's not alone and figure out how we can help protect him."

Jeremiah and Mark exchanged a look.

"We're not entirely certain he's going to continue to be in danger," Mark finally said.

"What makes you think that?" Cindy asked.

"Jeremiah and I were speculating that the attack on him might have been more about luring us here than actually killing him."

Cindy was silent for a few seconds as she thought about that. Finally, she shook her head.

"Either way, we have to go see him."

"Until we have a better idea of the scope of Matthews' network or influence, we're going to need to take similar precautions when we go anywhere," Mark said.

"So, it takes us longer to get places. That doesn't mean we just sit here. We came to see Gerald and that's precisely what I'm going to do," Cindy said.

~

It was evening by the time Cindy and Mark reached the hospital. They'd left the others back at the hotel to strategize. Joseph had been right. Their adversary would be looking for groups of six, so two could travel together and have a greater chance of going undetected, particularly if they used only cash when dealing with taxis.

Jeremiah had wanted to accompany Cindy, but ultimately it had been decided that it was better if he stayed and did what he could to secure their rooms at the new hotel. Besides, if the police gave Cindy any trouble it would be easier for Mark to smooth it over.

There was an officer standing guard outside Gerald's room, but he already knew to expect Cindy and Mark. After showing him their identification, they went inside.

Cindy's chest tightened as she entered the hospital room. Gerald was pale and eerily thin. Cindy reminded herself that he'd been in a coma for nearly two years. He smiled when he saw her, and even that movement looked difficult. The nurse who was checking his vitals helped him sit up. His emaciated arms shook with the effort.

"Thank you," he said, his voice thin and raspy.

The nurse nodded but didn't say anything. She kept her back to Cindy and Mark as she changed Gerald's IV.

"Gerald, I'm so glad you're awake," Cindy said, tears unexpectedly filling her eyes and rolling down her cheeks.

"You don't look glad," he said.

"It's just…"

"I know. I'm a sight. Don't worry, though, it's just muscle atrophy. I'll be right as rain with some physical therapy," he said.

She nodded, not trusting her voice in that moment.

The nurse ducked her head and left the room, giving the three of them some privacy.

"Of course, I was a bit surprised to discover how long I'd been out of it," Gerald said.

"I'm so sorry he did this to you," she said.

"Me, too. I take it that you figured out what I was trying to tell you when I was attacked?"

“We assume you were trying to tell us that Matthews is alive.”

“Yes,” he said.

“We’re guessing he’s the one who attacked you yesterday after you woke up,” Cindy said.

“Beats me. I was asleep when it happened. Can you imagine that? Been asleep for all that time and I wasn’t awake ten minutes before I fell asleep again. At least it was on my own terms. Anyway, I woke up because I couldn’t breathe. Someone was trying to smother me with a pillow. I was too weak to fight back, but fortunately they were monitoring some of my vital signs so when the machines started sending up alarms everyone came running.”

“Thank heavens,” Cindy said.

“I’m glad you’re here. There’s some stuff I didn’t get a chance to tell you before I was attacked and ended up in the coma.”

“Like what?” Cindy asked, leaning closer.

~

Something was wrong. Mark knew it in his gut. He was trying to place his finger on what exactly it could be.

He knew Gerald was about to tell them something important, but he couldn’t get his mind to focus on it. The nurse, there was something wrong with the nurse. She had kept her face mostly away from them, but he’d caught a glimpse of her profile as she left. It had seemed familiar to him.

“Gerald, what’s in the IV?” Mark asked, interrupting.

“Nutrients and fluids mostly. I’m supposed to start trying to eat soft food again tomorrow. Why?”

“Did you recognize that nurse?”

“Yes, she was here yesterday.”

In a flash it came to him. Mark hadn’t seen her before, but he had seen someone who looked exactly like her—her twin sister who had been killed right in front of him.

“Stop that IV!” he screamed at Cindy as he turned and ran out the door.

5

"How's it going?" Joseph asked Jeremiah.

Jeremiah looked up at him. "I'm almost done."

"It's a little late to ask, but is there anything I can do to help?"

"Short of hiring an unstoppable, unbribable team of bodyguards, nothing comes to mind," he said with a wry smile.

"I actually know just the guys," Joseph said, his face inscrutable.

"You know, with a poker face like that, you would have made one heck of a spy."

"Who says I'm not?"

I do. You're too nice, Jeremiah thought.

"So, do you think we're safe?" Joseph asked.

"For now. I think it's going to take a while for him to track us. Of course, it depends on just how many connections he has in this city and how loyal they are to him."

"If he's bought their loyalty, I can outbid him," Joseph said grimly. "I'm fairly confident the manager here is in our corner now. I also dangled the possibility of more money if he discovers anyone asking about us."

"Hopefully that will do it. Unfortunately, you can't bribe the entire city or even really know which people to target. We just don't have enough information."

"True," Joseph said. "While I can continue to grease the obvious palms, we need to think of other possible solutions. After all, money will only take us so far. Some people can't be bought. At least, not easily."

"Yes, if they're loyal to him because he earned it or has terrified them into giving it, that's an entirely different story. I like this room and this hotel, though. If we have to stay in a hotel, this is a good one."

"I'm glad you approve. I like it, but frankly I'd stay in a complete dive if it meant staying safe."

Jeremiah shook his head. "All we can do at this point is be careful and smart and try to stay a step ahead of Matthews and whoever he has working for him."

"Do you think he's really here, in the city?"

Jeremiah nodded slowly. He had nothing to base it on except for years of carefully honed instincts.

"Any man who would set himself up as a cult leader has enough of an ego that I think he'd want to be present for whatever scheme of his is about to play out," Jeremiah said.

"I don't like it," Joseph said. "I feel like he has the home field advantage."

"He does. Hopefully we can even the odds a little bit. At least we've got a base of operations now that is fairly secure."

"You know we're lucky that Mardi Gras is still almost two weeks away. Otherwise, we would have had more difficulty getting a hotel room at this or any other place."

"City still seems pretty crowded," Jeremiah muttered.

There had been more hotel guests milling about in the lobby than he would have liked. On the one hand, the more people the easier it was for them to walk around unnoticed.

On the other, it meant that he had a lot more people to keep an eye on as their enemy also had a lot of cover and could have accomplices anywhere.

"Well, it is Carnival season. Mardi Gras is just the last day of the season. There are parades, parties, and balls going on all the time. There'll be quite a number this weekend starting on Friday."

It was Wednesday. That didn't give them much time to figure out what was going on before things got even crazier than they already were.

"You ever been here during Carnival?" he asked Joseph.

The other man nodded. "I came for a weekend during college with some of my dormmates. It was…crazy."

"You don't seem the type to willingly participate in some of the…overindulgence."

"Designated driver. Plus, with the guys I knew, someone had to be prepared with bail money. I did have some fun. Admittedly it was mostly at my friends' expense."

"So noted," Jeremiah said, raising an eyebrow.

Joseph smirked but didn't elaborate.

~

Mark felt like he was chasing a ghost as he raced out of the hospital room.

"Which way did the nurse go?" he asked the startled police officer.

The man pointed to the left and Mark sprinted down the hall.

He had just seen Sadie Colbert, the real Sadie, the one who had been kidnapped by Matthews' cult as a child. She looked just like her twin, the woman who had given birth to Not Paul's son. The hair was different, the face was younger, less worn and aged, but the profile was identical.

As he ran down the corridor, his mind raced ahead. He had no idea if she actually worked at the hospital or had instead stolen or borrowed the nurse's uniform. If it was the former, she might just return to her duties like nothing was wrong, not knowing that Mark had recognized her. If that was the case, then he should be speaking to the charge nurse. If it was the latter, then she would be smart to have left immediately and he should be heading for the parking lot if he hoped to catch her.

Normally he would have gone straight to the parking lot, but Gerald had said that the nurse had been there the day before as well. Mark turned and headed for the nursing station.

~

Cindy hit the call button before grabbing hold of the IV line that was going into Gerald's wrist. She didn't want to try to remove it from him and she didn't know how to stop the drip of liquid from the bag hanging on the pole. She did the only thing she could think of and bent the tube in half. Putting a crimp in it effectively stopped the flow of liquid.

The door opened and the policeman stuck his head inside.

"Are you okay?" he asked.

"No! Get a doctor or a nurse, someone. I think he might have been poisoned!"

The officer disappeared and she heard him shouting a second later. Within a minute two nurses and a doctor were in the room.

"What's happening?" the doctor demanded.

"We have reason to believe that there's been another attempt on this man's life," Cindy said, trying to be clear and articulate. "We believe someone masquerading as a nurse is trying to administer some sort of poison via this IV. My friend, a detective, is chasing down the suspect. He asked me to stop the IV and this is what I did," she said, indicating the crimped tube.

"Smart thinking," the doctor said as he moved forward to have a look at it. He clamped off the tube, stopping the flow of liquid. "Okay, you can let go now."

Cindy did as instructed, relieved to see that the liquid had indeed stopped flowing.

"How long was it running?"

"Two minutes or less," Cindy said.

The doctor began barking orders and the nurses scrambled. Cindy backed into the far corner by the window where she'd be out of the way but could still watch what was happening. At this point she had no intention of leaving Gerald's side until she knew he was out of danger.

~

Mark made it to the nurses' station and could tell by the look on the charge nurse's face that his appearance frightened her.

"I'm looking for a nurse," he said. "She was just in to see Gerald Wilson. She was also in his room yesterday."

As he described her, the nurse began to nod her head.

"You're looking for Mary Smith. She's new here. She just started yesterday."

"Where is she?" Mark asked.

"She should be making her rounds. Let me check her schedule. After Mr. Wilson she sees Mrs. Orion in Room 412."

"Where is that?"

The nurse pointed. Mark turned to look and at that moment he saw Sadie Colbert step out of the room and into the hall. Mark took off at a sprint. Sadie saw him coming, spun and ran.

He closed the distance remaining and reached for her red hair. He grabbed hold of it, and it came off in his hand. He stumbled slightly and he realized that she'd been wearing a wig. Sadie began to laugh maniacally as she twisted and threw the clipboard she was holding at his face.

Mark barely managed to dodge it, the hard plastic edge scraping his cheek. He thought about dropping the wig but realized he could get a DNA sample off it if he couldn't catch Sadie. So, he kept clutching it as he chased her down the corridor. She made a sudden turn down another hallway to the left.

Mark heard a crash as he barreled around it and a moment later found himself flat on his back, staring up at the ceiling. He'd had the wind knocked out of him. He struggled to breathe for a couple of seconds before he forced himself to sit up. He looked and saw that there were fifty ball point pens scattered all over the floor amidst the remains of a broken glass container that Sadie had clearly pushed off the counter she had run past. The pens had rolled beneath his feet, knocking him down.

There was no sign of Sadie. He hauled himself to his feet and grabbed a nurse that was rushing forward to help him.

"I need this entire building locked down, no one in or out. A nurse just attempted to murder a patient," he said.

He dug his badge out of his pocket and flashed it. He didn't have jurisdiction here, but the shiny gold badge had the effect he intended it to. The nurse scrambled to the nearest phone and began shouting instructions.

He started walking down the hallway, glancing left and right as he passed rooms. He pulled his phone out and called Detective Lewis.

"Hello, this is Detective Lorraine Lewis," she said when she answered after the second ring.

"Hi, this is Detective Mark Walters."

"I didn't expect to hear from you again so soon."

"Well, I'm at the hospital where Gerald is at. Someone here who is either a nurse or masquerading as one just tried to kill him. I've asked for the hospital to be locked down so we can find her."

There was a pause and then a soft sigh. "You do like to make a mess, don't you?" she asked.

"Yes, Ma'am," he said before hanging up.

~

Cindy saw a security guard run past the door in the direction Mark had headed. She hoped they were going to help him because he had caught the nurse. Thirty seconds later she saw a different group of guards head in the opposite direction and she grew confused.

Mark probably alerted security to help him search, she realized after a moment.

She turned back and looked at Gerald. He was still awake and very, very anxious looking as the nurses worked on him. They needed to know what had been in the IV to know how to treat him. The doctor had immediately sent it for tests but that might take too long.

The woman who had poisoned him almost certainly knew what she'd used. As much as Cindy wanted to stay and watch out for Gerald, she realized she could do him more good if she joined the search for the woman who had done this to him.

"I'll be back shortly. I promise," she said to him on her way out of the room.

She looked up and down the hall for a moment, debating which way to go.

Please, God, protect us all, she prayed. And help us stop those who would harm us.

She took a deep breath and moved to the right.

~

Mark winced, his back throbbing as he moved slowly down the hallway. Scattering the pens on the ground that way had been diabolically effective. It was going to be uncomfortable for a few days. He was getting tired of getting injured in the line of duty, or, as too often seemed to be the case lately, injured while off duty. He dreaded having to explain to Traci that he'd gotten hurt again. It always worried her so much.

He kept walking even though his hopes of catching Sadie had dwindled. If he was lucky, she was still in the building, and she'd be trapped there until New Orleans police could capture her. If he wasn't, then she was long gone.

As he turned and saw movement in a darkened room to his left, he realized there was a third option. He could be very, very unlucky and the woman he was hunting could be staring at him with a deranged smile while she aimed a gun at his head.

6

"Markie, Markie, Markie. What am I going to do with you?" Sadie asked in a singsong voice that sent a shiver down Mark's spine.

"For starters, Sadie, you can put down the gun and tell me where to find Matthews," he said, keeping his voice even.

She tilted her head to the side and wrinkled up her nose, looking like a little girl.

"No, I don't think so," she said.

"Okay, how about just putting down the gun?"

"Because little girls like me shouldn't be allowed to play with loaded weapons?" she asked, still in that little girl voice.

"Something like that," he said, wondering how he could possibly get the gun away from her without her shooting him first.

"It's okay. I know how. Papa taught us."

"You and Sandra?" he asked.

She frowned at him. "No, silly. Papa taught us. I'm the best, though. He says I'm his little sharpshooter."

"Papa, you mean Matthews, the man who kidnapped you?" Mark asked.

"He didn't kidnap me. He saw how special I was and took me to live with him," she said, eyes big and shiny, almost doll-like.

Bile rose in the back of Mark's throat and he swallowed.

"Why don't we go see your Papa," Mark suggested.

"No. He's not ready for company yet. He has to get the place all clean and fixed up."

"Okay, I'll go visit when he's done with that. Be a good girl and remind me of the address, though. I forgot to bring it with me."

She laughed. "You're so silly. Papa said you were, but you're so much sillier than I thought."

"Why is that, sweetheart?" he asked, trying to appease her while he figured out how to get the gun.

"You're here."

He glanced around. "You mean, the hospital?"

His heart began pounding even harder as he contemplated the thought that Matthews might be close.

"No, here."

"In the room?" he asked, starting to wonder if maybe he had mistaken her meaning and she had a separate personality that she thought of as Papa.

She rolled her eyes and giggled again. "New Orleans, silly."

"Of course, you're right. I am silly," Mark said, smiling broadly as he took a slow step forward.

"Bad, Markie," she said, cocking the gun as she took a step back. "Mustn't do that."

He froze. She hadn't shot him yet so there was a chance that she didn't intend to. However, he believed that if he pushed, she absolutely would.

He took a slow step back and she stepped forward.

It's like a dance, he thought.

"So, when do I get to visit Papa?"

"At the party. Make sure you have your invitation. No one gets in without their invitation."

"I haven't received one," he said.

She smiled even more broadly.

"Oh, don't worry. You're on the list. I've seen it. You will get your invitation."

Mark felt sick inside as he wondered just what form this invitation would take.

"How do I know the post office will know where to deliver it to me?" he asked. At this point he was stalling for time while he tried to get something, anything out of her that could be useful.

"Papa doesn't use the mail. He says it lacks a personal touch. And don't worry. He knows where you are. That's his job. He's the King of New Orleans."

"Then that must make you a princess," Mark said.

"Uh huh."

"Well, your highness, did you already buy your dress for the party at one of the nice stores?"

"No, Papa had it made for me. It's beautiful. It's purple. That's my favorite color."

"Oh, mine, too," Mark said. "Who else is going to be at the party?"

"Some of Papa's friends. Some of them are very important."

"And are your brothers and sisters going to be there?"

"Some of them," she said, scowling slightly.

"But none of them are as important as you. You're the favorite."

"Of course, I am."

"So, he must tell you things he doesn't tell the others. Give you big responsibilities."

"Of course. He sent me to see you."

Mark blinked.

"To see me? When?"

"Today."

"Why didn't you say anything when we were both in Mr. Wilson's room?"

She shrugged. "Papa said not to bother. He said you'd follow me and then we could talk without the nosy woman overhearing."

"How did you know how to change Mr. Wilson's IV, his liquid?" Mark asked, wondering how the grown woman with the voice and language of a little girl had managed to pass herself off as a nurse for the last two days let alone have the knowledge to poison someone.

"That was easy. Father taught me how."

"He teaches you a lot, doesn't he?"

She nodded.

"I bet he tells you a lot of secrets, too."

"I know where it's hidden."

"Where what's hidden?"

"I saw him hide it."

Mark wasn't sure what she was talking about, but it didn't sound good.

"Where did he hide it?"

"At Green Pastures. I know where he hid it."

"You mean… the bodies?" he asked.

"No. The treasure."

There had long been speculation about what happened to the cult's wealth when it disappeared. Was it possible she was talking about that?

"How much treasure?" Mark asked.

"Enough for three kings and Papa is just one king," she confided.

"Who…who are the other two kings?"

Before she could answer he heard a man call. "Sir, are you alright? Sir, can you please turn around?"

Mark turned his head slightly and saw a security guard walking toward him.

"I'm fine," Mark called, trying to reassure the man.

He'd been hoping it was a police officer, but he didn't know if they were even at the hospital yet.

"Sir, I'm going to need you to vacate this hallway," the guard said, continuing to come toward him.

"I'm a police officer," Mark said. "And I can assure you, I'm fine right where I am."

"Someone is naughty," Sadie whispered, wiggling slightly from side to side as if so excited she could barely control herself.

"No, no one is naughty," Mark said as softly as he could.

"That's okay. I like it when they're naughty. Even if Papa doesn't."

The guard stepped closer.

Sadie's finger tightened on the trigger and she fired.

Mark heard the bullet whistle past him. He instinctively dropped to the floor. A second later the guard fell beside him, a neat round hole in the center of his forehead, his eyes fixed and staring.

"You didn't have to shoot him!" Mark said, anger filling him.

"No, but it was easier and more fun."

"Fun? Little missy, you're going to earn yourself a spanking," Mark said, reminding himself that he was dealing with a childlike personality. He also realized that when others heard the shot and came running she could hurt a lot more people. He had to stop her and there was only one thing he could think of.

He turned and looked up at her and saw that she looked a little startled at the suggestion. He stood slowly, deliberately, to his feet and held out his hand.

“Give me the gun,” he said sternly.

She blinked at him and a look of confusion swept across her face.

“Young lady, I’m going to count to three.”

“One.”

He was bluffing, but he was hoping that she didn’t know that she held all the power in the situation.

She made a little whimpering sound in her throat.

“Two,” he said, taking a risk and moving a step closer.

“I don’t want to,” she whispered.

“This is not about what you want. Don’t make me say three. You know what will happen if I do.”

She thrust the gun into his hand and he pulled it back in relief. He quickly turned it around on her.

“Now, let’s go have a little chat with Papa,” he said.

Her demeanor changed back swiftly from the frightened child to the capricious one.

“I told you. Not now.”

He motioned with the gun.

She shook her head.

“It won’t work to wave the gun at me.”

“Why not? You aren’t afraid?” Mark asked.

“Of course not, silly,” she said, all smiles and laughter again.

“And why not?”

"Because I only ever carry one bullet."

Mark quickly examined the gun and saw that she was right. He looked back up at her in surprise.

"You only need one. More make you sloppy."

"Who… who were you supposed to shoot with that bullet?" Mark asked.

Sadie smiled. "Daddy told me I could shoot anyone but you or that nosy lady. It would spoil the party if I did."

"But he told you that you could kill anyone else?" Mark asked.

"Of course. I'm his favorite. That means he lets me do all kinds of fun things. He also lets me choose all the time," Sadie said as she backed farther into the room.

"Choose what?" Mark asked as he followed.

They were in the middle of an empty, darkened patient room. There was a window on the far side letting in some light and she was steadily backing toward it as she talked.

"Pizza toppings. Cartoons. I even get to help pick where we go on vacation sometimes."

"Well, it's my turn to choose where you and I go," Mark said.

"Not this time. It will be your turn next time," Sadie said.

She opened the window and hopped up on the windowsill.

He wanted to lunge forward and grab her, but there was something that told him to hold back. She could easily have another weapon on her, and this was just a ploy to pull him in close. He could hear running footsteps coming his way.

"She's in here, trying to go out the window!" he shouted.

He tossed the gun onto the bed so that whoever burst through the doorway wouldn't see him holding a gun and start shooting by mistake.

"I've enjoyed playing with you, Markie," Sadie said with a giggle.

"Sadie, there's some things I have to tell you. Your family is looking for you."

Of course, he knew that her family were all dead, well, except for her sister's son whom she'd never met but he was deathly afraid she might already know about.

She shook her head.

"Papa knows right where I am."

"No, I mean your actual parents, your mother and father, and your sister, Sandra."

"Liar, liar, pants on fire," she said. "They're all dead so they can't be looking for me. And I wouldn't want them to even if they could."

"Why not?" Mark asked, hearing shouts as people saw the guard on the ground.

She straightened slightly and looked him in the eyes. It took him aback for a moment.

"Because I belong to Papa."

"He stole you."

"You're wrong."

"How can you say that?" Mark asked, frustration welling within him. There had to be a way to reach her.

She spoke again and Sadie's voice shifted and sounded suddenly more adult. Her smile changed as well, no longer the broad, joyous smile of a child but ruthless, cunning.

"Because I chose him."

Then she tumbled backward through the window.

7

Mark started to lunge forward, but someone tackled him from behind.

"Get the girl! She attacked Gerald and killed the guard!" he shouted. "She just went out the window."

They were on the second floor which meant she could have landed safely if she knew how to jump. However, the odd backward flip she'd done out the window had him puzzled.

He felt the cold steel of handcuffs snapping onto his wrists.

"Found the gun!" someone shouted.

"Forget the gun! Get the girl! I mean, woman!" he said, correcting himself at the end. Talking to her it had been hard to see her as an adult woman and not an eight-year-old girl.

Except at the end when her voice and demeanor changed.

He shuddered. She scared him in a way very few things ever had.

"What's going on here? Let him go!" he heard a woman shout.

Cindy, right on time, he thought.

"Someone killed Wally," a man said.

"He's a police detective. It wasn't him. It was the fake nurse that he was chasing who attempted to murder a patient in front of us."

"Is this lady telling the truth? Are you a detective?"

"My badge is in my pocket," Mark said. "I'm the one who called for the lockdown to keep the woman who just went out the window from getting away!"

He heard swearing and then someone hauled to him his feet and uncuffed him. He ran to the window and looked down. Below there was a stack of old mattresses piled up next to a dumpster. It would have been easy for Sadie to fall out the window and land on them.

He turned to Cindy who was staring at him wide-eyed and pointedly keeping her back toward the dead body in the hall.

"She planned this. All of this. She planned on me chasing her. She planned to be caught in this room."

"Why?" Cindy asked.

"To send a message."

"What message?"

"That Matthews is in control."

~

Jeremiah's phone rang.

"It's Cindy," he told the others. He'd been beginning to wonder when he was going to hear from her or Mark.

"Hey. Everything okay?" he asked.

"It is now. We'll tell you the whole story when we get back home."

"Okay," Jeremiah said.

"It's going to take us a while to get there."

"Do you need me to come get you?"

"No, we can manage. I love you."

"Love you, too."

Jeremiah hung up then looked at Traci, Joseph, and Geanie. "Well, they had trouble."

"Pay up," Geanie said, turning to Joseph.

"Wait, not until we find out what type of trouble they had," Joseph said.

"Are either of them injured?" Traci asked anxiously.

"She didn't say."

"Then probably not," Joseph said, taking out his wallet and handing money to Traci.

"What's going on?" Jeremiah asked.

Traci looked at him sheepishly. "While you were busy safeguarding us, we were busy wagering on what was happening with Mark and Cindy."

"We know it was wrong. Sorry," Geanie mumbled.

Jeremiah smirked. "You didn't let me in on the action?"

"I told you he'd be cool with it," Joseph crowed.

Both women opened their purses and handed him money.

Truth be told Jeremiah had seen people cope with life-and-death situations in far more destructive or morbid ways. He was glad they had found a way to make it better for themselves.

Now he just needed to find a way to make this whole situation better for all of them. It had become increasingly clear that they had walked right into a trap. The smart thing to do would be to turn around and go straight home, but he had a feeling that wasn't going to satisfy anyone, particularly Cindy. She would want to see justice done.

So would Mark. After all, he was even more invested in what was happening here than Cindy was.

Plus, he knew men like Matthews. Once he'd put a target on them, he wouldn't be satisfied until he'd destroyed them or vice versa. There was really no walking away from this. The question then became how to level the playing field when he had clear home field advantage.

The more Jeremiah thought about it, the more convinced he was that they were in trouble. The man had had nearly two years to plan what would happen when Gerald came out of a coma or he used some other means to entice them to his city. They'd had less than a day's notice that they were even going to New Orleans.

Jeremiah also knew that the best laid plans could be upset by an adversary who was determined, committed, and creative. Cindy was determined to take down Matthews. Mark was completely committed to it. That left Jeremiah to be creative in how they got it done.

It was times like this when he missed having the resources of the Mossad at his disposal. He thought about his CIA ally, Martin. He could reach out and see if he could get some help there. Working with Martin, though, came with its own share of difficulties. Best to leave that as Plan C.

Now to come up with Plans A and B, he thought wryly.

~

It took four hours, five different modes of transportation, and an exhausting conversation with the police for Cindy and Mark to make it back to the hotel. When they got there, they went straight to Mark, Traci, Joseph, and Geanie's room. Everyone was there waiting for them.

Cindy threw her arms around Jeremiah and he hugged her tight.

"I'm glad you're okay," he whispered for her ears alone.

She nodded.

"Me, too."

As many dead bodies as she'd seen she would have thought she'd get used to it, but she didn't. It had been horrible coming upon the scene and seeing the guard lying dead on the floor. Even worse were the thoughts running through her head that kept making her wonder if she'd left Gerald's room just two or three minutes earlier if there was something she could have done to help, to save him.

She knew that "what ifs" and "could haves" lined the road to insanity, but every time something like this happened, she still had to beat them back. And in the darkest moments when she found that hard, she would remind herself that yes, she could have gone earlier and what if she or Mark had been killed instead because she changed the circumstances.

She let go of Jeremiah and sat down on the couch. He sat on the arm of it and left a hand on her back, gently stroking up and down her spine. She had no idea how he knew to do that, but it was incredibly soothing and she could slowly feel the knots in her stomach releasing.

"So, what happened?" Geanie asked, leaning forward and looking from Cindy to Mark and back again.

"You remember Sadie Colbert, the girl that the cult kidnapped? Her twin took her name and ended up being the mother of Not Paul's kid? You know, the woman who was shot right in front of me by a sniper?" Mark asked.

Traci looked at him like he was crazy. "Um, yeah, a little hard to forget that," she said.

Mark gave a short, barking laugh. “I know. I try to all the time.”

“If I remember correctly, her body was never recovered and Not Paul told her sister that he didn’t know for sure what had happened to her,” Joseph said.

“That’s correct. Well, I now know what’s happened to her.”

“What?” Traci asked.

“She’s alive and well in New Orleans working for the same psychopath that kidnapped her.”

“Get out!” Geanie exclaimed.

“Yeah. I spent I don’t know how long talking to her. I have to say that ‘mentally unstable’ doesn’t even begin to cover it. Her voice and her body language for almost the entire conversation were that of a child and she consistently referred to Matthews as Papa.”

“That’s disturbing,” Joseph said.

“I can’t even imagine,” Traci said, looking distressed.

Mark shifted in his seat and winced.

“Do they have ice machines here?” he asked. “Or can they send some up?”

“Why?” Traci asked.

“I hurt my back when I fell. Crazy woman dumped like fifty ballpoint pens on the ground. I’m going to be stiff for a few days.”

Traci sighed, walked over to her purse, and took money out. She then walked back and handed it to Joseph who tucked it into his pocket.

“What just happened?” Mark asked.

“You don’t want to know,” Jeremiah told him.

“I’ll call down and have some ice packs sent up,” Joseph said, heading to the phone.

A minute later the ice had been ordered.

"How did you even find this woman?" Geanie asked.

"Funny thing," Cindy said. "She was trying to kill Gerald."

That elicited an outburst from everyone.

She held up her hand. "He's okay. She was masquerading as a nurse. She switched out his IV, and as she was leaving the room Mark got a good look at her and realized who she was. I put a crimp in the IV line until the doctor could get there. Luckily they were able to figure out pretty quickly what she'd given him."

"They ran chemical tests on it?" Jeremiah guessed.

"Eventually. They figured it out faster by doing a quick inventory of the restricted drugs and they discovered what was missing."

"Wow, that's scary," Traci said. "To think, if you guys hadn't acted that fast he could have been dead in minutes. It's lucky you got a good look at her, Hon."

"I don't think luck had anything to do with it," Mark said.

"How do you figure?" Joseph asked.

"I'm not convinced she was trying to kill Gerald," Mark said.

Cindy saw Jeremiah lean forward sharply at that.

"Why?" he asked.

"Because if that was her goal, she would have done it a lot faster and simpler. Heck, she was even masquerading as his nurse yesterday so she could have killed him before we even got to the state. No, I think poisoning him was just a ruse to get me to follow her, to let us know that Matthews is calling the shots and orchestrating everything. I'm telling you the timing of everything, she had it planned. She even lured me to the room she had chosen to escape from."

"She killed a hospital security guard," Cindy said quietly.

"Yeah," Mark said, bitterness edging into his voice. "She held a gun on me for five minutes and I believed she was going to kill me. Turned out that wasn't her plan at all."

Cindy couldn't help but wonder if he felt guilty as well, like there was more he could have done to save the guy.

"She did kill someone. She could have killed you, too," Cindy said.

He shook his head slowly. "No. She only had one bullet and she knew it. The way she talked about it, too. She had it for fun or an emergency, but not for me. She's a sharpshooter, that's what she said Matthews calls her. And I can testify that she nailed that guy between the eyes without any problem whatsoever. And she didn't have to. She just wanted to."

Traci moved to sit next to Mark and she took his hand and began to massage it. "I'm so sorry."

"Thanks."

"Why didn't she want you dead?" Geanie asked. "I mean, I'm grateful, but I don't understand what the whole point of that was."

"To scare and intimidate," Jeremiah said slowly. "Matthews put us on notice that he can get to us anytime, anywhere, and that he's just waiting."

"Yeah. Apparently, he wants a face-to-face. I guess it's been a long time coming," Mark said.

"Any idea where or when this is supposed to happen?" Joseph asked.

"All I know is Little Miss Crazy Pants said that he was the King of New Orleans and that he was going to throw a party. My invitation is apparently on its way, but not by mail because that's not personal enough."

"I shudder to think what his idea of personal is," Joseph said.

"Don't bother trying to think about it. I'm sure we're going to find out soon enough," Mark said grimly. "There's something else," he said, glancing at Cindy.

Cindy nodded. "She indicated that Matthews wants me at the party, too."

Jeremiah wanted to say that was never going to happen, but he knew better. One way or another this monstrous performance was going to play out. He was just counting on Matthews to not realize he had chosen to tangle with the wrong man until it was too late.

There was a sudden knock on the door.

"Room service," a muffled voice said.

"That will be the ice," Joseph said, standing up.

Jeremiah got up and intercepted him.

"Be sure," he warned the other man.

Joseph checked the peephole and nodded. He opened the door. A young bellman, scarcely more than a boy, stood there holding an elaborate ice bucket bearing the hotel's crest on it.

"Is there anything else I can bring up for you?" the boy asked eagerly after Joseph handed him a tip.

"Not right now."

The boy nodded and left the room. Joseph carried the ice bucket over to the table. He removed the lid and backpedaled.

Cindy jumped to her feet and pushed forward to see what was wrong. An icy hand of fear wrapped around her heart as she stared down into the bucket. There, nestled on top of the cubes, was another mask made out of skin.

There was a clearly visible note next to it and she read it in a shaking voice.

"Peek-a-boo, I see you."

8

Jeremiah moved forward quickly and took a good look at the mask.

"How did he find us already?" Cindy asked with a gasp.

"We need to grab that bellboy," Mark said, heading for the door.

"Why?" Jeremiah asked.

"Because he brought it."

"He's either innocent and won't be able to tell us anything, or he's another one of Matthew's operatives, in which case he already had an escape route mapped out."

"We have to change hotels," Joseph said.

"We should go home," Traci chimed in.

"No, it's a waste of time to do anything until we find out how he's tracking us," Jeremiah said.

"Tracking us?" Joseph asked.

Jeremiah nodded. "He wants us to think he's all powerful, all-seeing," he said, gesturing to the mask. "That he has eyes and ears everywhere. What's far more likely is that he's planted a tracker somewhere in our luggage. He probably had someone at the airport or the last hotel or the driver for the car service do it. Until we find it, he's going to know our every move the moment we do."

That was why the bug in the first hotel had been so obvious. Hide something in plain sight so everyone feels like they found it and now everything is okay. Or get them to tear apart the rooms searching for more when all along they had brought the real tracker with them. It was smart, insidious.

He's a master at psychological warfare. Well, two can play that game.

"Mark, call Detective Lewis and let her know about this. Joseph, check with room service about that bell boy. Let's figure out if he works for the hotel or for Matthews. Geanie, Traci, it's almost midnight and none of us has eaten. There's a twenty-four hour diner a block from here. Walk there, order food, bring it straight back. If anyone hassles you-"

"Hit them in the Adam's Apple," Geanie interrupted.

He nodded.

He turned to Cindy. "You and I are going to find that tracker."

Everyone scattered to their various assigned tasks. Jeremiah led Cindy across the hall to their room.

"We'll search our luggage first," he said.

"What are we looking for?"

"Anything that you didn't pack yourself, no matter how small. We could be looking for something like a button. Doublecheck all your clothes to make sure there's nothing different about them than when you packed them, check pockets, loose buttons, tags, hems. See if anything feels different, like something was sewn into a lining."

Cindy's eyes bugged out of her head.

"Whoever did this likely wouldn't have had time to sew it in, but we need to be thorough anyway."

"Got it," she said.

She went to work tearing apart her suitcase. While he checked his own, he spared an occasional glance for her and was pleased to see that she was carefully examining everything. At one point he glanced over while she was examining a bra and he quickly looked away, feeling himself flush slightly.

"Make sure you check your toiletries just as carefully," he said.

"You think he put a tracker in my toothpaste?" she said, clearly trying to make him smile.

"Stranger things have happened," he said.

She bit her lip and nodded then continued combing through her things.

He finished first and was about to suggest he help her finish checking her bags when there was a knock on the door. He checked the peephole before answering.

"It's Joseph," he said.

He opened the door and Joseph came in.

"Mark called Detective Lewis and she and her partner are on their way. I called downstairs and found out the boy who brought up the ice bucket is legit. He's the nephew of the manager. The person in charge swore she filled the ice bucket with ice cubes and that was it. It sat for about four minutes before the boy was free to run it up here. There were a lot of people in and out. Any of them could have tampered with it. So, you were definitely right to send the ladies out to get dinner."

Jeremiah nodded. "We're finished here. We need to go through all the luggage in the other room. I can walk you through what you're looking for."

"I'd feel better if you did it. I wouldn't want to be responsible for missing something and putting us all in danger," Joseph admitted.

"Fair enough. We'll take care of it."

The three of them moved back to the first room. Cindy volunteered a single strand of hair and Jeremiah positioned it in the door lock in such a way that he'd be able to tell instantly if someone had entered their room.

Mark was on the phone with Liam. He was having him run a check to see if there had been any incidents of body mutilation around the time that Matthews' cult operated in Green Pastures. From the look on the detective's face it was clear he knew it was a longshot, but Jeremiah got that the other man needed to feel like he was doing something.

Jeremiah and Cindy moved to the bedroom.

"You check the girls' luggage. I'll check the guys'."

"Makes sense. I'm guessing you don't want to go pawing at someone else's delicates," she said with a small smile.

He smiled back. "If I was going to paw at anyone's delicates, trust me they would have been yours."

"I should hope so."

She was scared. He knew her well enough to tell, but she was clearly putting a lot of effort into making sure she didn't let it overwhelm her. That was why she was teasing and making the small jokes. Normally he would have really appreciated it, but he was very focused.

It's because I'm scared for her, for Mark, for all of them.

He just kept praying that they wouldn't have to use the things he'd taught them, but that if they did they would remember their training and use it to maximum affect.

He started going through Joseph's suitcase while Cindy was going through Geanie's. When he got to Joseph's toiletry kit he found what he was looking for. A small, flat disc had been stuck to the bottom of his can of shaving cream. It had been adhered in such a fashion that the can would still stand flat on the counter.

Jeremiah pulled it free then moved to the bathroom where he filled a glass of water.

"Cindy, bring me a high heel shoe," he called.

Cindy returned a moment later with a pair of leopard print heels that had to belong to Geanie. He grabbed one shoe and drove the heel down on the tracker. He heard a satisfying crack as the casing was damaged. He handed the shoe back to Cindy then dropped the tracker into the glass of water. It sparked for a moment.

"So, that's it?" Cindy asked.

He nodded. "We'll toss it in the hotel trash, but it's gone."

"So, we can stop searching?"

He shook his head. "We keep going just in case they planted more than one."

When they had finished with Joseph and Geanie's luggage, they started on Mark and Traci's. They were almost finished, and Jeremiah was starting to think there was nothing left to find, when Cindy held something up.

"This is odd," she said.

He turned to look. It was a small flip phone. With a frown he took it from Cindy and examined it.

"I thought Traci used a smart phone," he said.

"She does and she's got it in the other room with her," Cindy confirmed.

"Then what's this doing here?" Jeremiah mused.

He opened the phone and checked it. There was no list of recent calls nor were there any stored numbers.

"It's a burner phone," he commented.

"Could that be used to track us?"

"Yes."

"You were right, they planted a second one."

Jeremiah shook his head. "I don't think so. After all, Traci would be sure to discover this if she unpacked."

"You think it's hers?" Cindy asked, taking it back and staring at it.

"Yes."

"What on earth would she need a burner phone for?"

"That's an excellent question," Jeremiah said quietly as he glanced toward the other room, making sure the others hadn't overheard what they were talking about. "To talk to someone without anyone else knowing. Something like this is used by criminals, double agents, people leading secret lives."

"Traci is none of those," Cindy said, rolling her eyes.

Something occurred to Jeremiah at that moment that for some reason never had before. He cursed himself for not having put together the connection, obvious as it was.

Too obvious, that's the problem, he thought.

"What is it?" Cindy asked, reading him like a book.

"What's Traci's maiden name?" he asked softly.

She frowned for a moment. "It's right there. Wait, her younger sister is Lizzie… Matthews. That's it. Traci's maiden name is… oh no."

Cindy sat down abruptly on the bed, her hand flying to her mouth.

"It's got to be a common name, right?" she asked after a moment. "It's a coincidence, that's all."

"Is it?" he asked.

"Oh no."

Cindy started shaking. He knelt down and took her hand in his.

"Look at me, we don't know anything, okay. Maybe it is a total coincidence and Traci isn't related to Matthews and Not Paul at all."

"Or maybe it's not," she whispered.

Jeremiah cleared his throat. He looked at the phone Cindy was still holding. He took it gently from her hand.

"This might have been planted here after all."

"Why? You said it yourself. It's too big, too obvious."

"Exactly. It could be designed to do something else entirely. It could have been planted to raise suspicion, sow the seeds of doubt, and create a rift between her and Mark or her and the group," he said.

"I don't feel good," Cindy said.

"I know what you mean."

He heard the door in the other room open.

"We're back with dinner!" Traci called out.

"We'll ask her if it's hers," Jeremiah said, meeting Cindy's eyes.

He stood up.

"And we met the detectives outside," Geanie called out.

Jeremiah grimaced and slipped the phone into his pocket. Its presence and purpose were best discussed after the detectives had conducted their business and left.

~

Mark glanced up as Jeremiah and Cindy walked into the main room. He didn't ask if they'd found anything. That could wait until the other detectives had gone.

"We ended up going to a Chinese restaurant a few doors down that Traci found," Geanie said. "The food smells good so fingers crossed."

Mark noticed that Jeremiah and Cindy exchanged a swift glance. He wasn't sure what it was about, but something in their demeanor made his hair stand on end.

Detective Lewis had already pulled on gloves and had a pair of tweezers at the ready. She approached the ice bucket and lifted the mask free using the tweezers. Mark stepped forward as Detective Lewis carefully turned the mask over. He expected to see more pictures of Cindy, but was instead shocked to see pictures of himself. There was a distinct difference, though. Cindy's pictures had all been taken from public sources such as newspaper articles, the church's website, and things like that.

The pictures of him were all private, some of them taken by immediate family and friends and two that were clearly surveillance photos taken inside his own home while he was unaware that he was being watched. Mark's eyes locked in on the one at the top right corner. It was him sitting on his couch in the middle of the night holding the twins.

"Sit down, Mark," Jeremiah said, his arm around Mark's shoulders.

"Where did he get those?" Mark asked. "How did he get those? Those are taken in my house."

"Sit down," Jeremiah said more firmly, and he tugged hard enough that Mark was forced to move with him or fall.

Jeremiah led Mark over to the couch and pushed him down next to Cindy.

"It's okay," Cindy said softly.

"No, it's not. He has pictures of me with my kids," Mark said. "He has cameras in my house. He's been spying on me, watching me."

Mark was starting to sweat profusely, and he felt like he was about to throw up.

"So, is dealing with you guys always a 24/7 kind of job?" Detective Moretti asked sarcastically.

Cindy lifted her chin. "You'd have to ask the Pine Springs police department."

"Yeah, well I'm looking at a representative of same," Moretti said as he stared hard at Mark.

Mark had no idea why the other man was staring at him. He did know that he had a nearly overwhelming urge to punch him in the nose.

Lorraine's phone rang and she answered it.

"Hello? Yes, Doctor. Wait. What's missing?"

She glanced at the ice bucket.

Mark frowned, wondering if this had something to do with this mask or the first one.

"How is that even possible?" Lorraine asked. "I see. How long ago? Yes, I have a pretty good idea. Keep me informed and I'll do the same."

"Trouble?" Mark asked when she had hung up the phone.

"Yes. It appears that someone took something from the guard who was killed at the hospital after he was transferred to the morgue."

"What was taken?" he asked.

"His face."

9

"Anyone else in the city been getting these human skin masks?" Mark asked.

"No, just the lot of you," Detective Lewis said with a scowl.

"Well, then, I think we can be fairly certain where this next one is going to turn up. Maybe this is the break we need, though. There must be cameras in the morgue or in the hallway outside."

"Ostensibly, they were disabled," she said crisply. "That was the first thing Dr. Westham checked."

"So, someone snuck in, surgically removed the face, then snuck out again, all in twenty minutes or less? Is that even possible?" Cindy asked.

"Yes," Jeremiah said.

Mark didn't know a lot at that moment, but he was absolutely certain that he didn't want to know how Jeremiah knew that. He still felt sick to the bottom of his soul. How long had Matthews been spying on his family?

"Paul, Not Paul, what have you done to me?" he whispered.

He didn't care that the other detectives were looking at him oddly. All he cared about was finding a way to put an end to Matthews' reign of terror.

Why did I have to be the one that ended up with Paul as a partner? Is God punishing me for something?

He was feeling trapped and desperate which wasn't a good combination. He was also seriously regretting the choice to come to New Orleans.

"Are you in distress Detective Walters? Your face has a distinct pallor about it that was not present earlier," Lorraine noted.

"Yes, I'm in distress. The surprise is that you're somehow shocked by that," he snapped.

"Easy, Mark," Jeremiah murmured.

"Yeah, Honey, just try to relax," Traci said.

He wanted so very badly to laugh at that. She hadn't seen what he had, otherwise she wouldn't be telling him to relax.

Which is a good thing, he reminded himself.

Seeing those pictures taken inside their house would freak her out.

"Have you discovered anything since we saw you earlier?" Jeremiah asked Lorraine.

As they had earlier, Lorraine was taking point in talking with them while her partner quietly snooped around.

Detective Lewis hesitated and Mark pounced on it.

"You have. What have you found?"

She sized him up and then Lorraine finally nodded her head slowly.

"We ran a rapid DNA test on the first mask and we got a hit."

"Whose… face… was it?" Cindy asked.

"The face belonged to a reporter from California, Felix Hoskins, who was killed two days ago."

"Felix Hoskins, I know that name," Cindy said.

"We all do," Mark said. "That was the reporter who stole the jury summons so he could sit on that murder trial with you."

"He was pretending to be a guy named Tanner," Cindy said, remembering.

"And I believe you were the arresting officer," Lorraine said pointedly to Mark. "Given the two masks I would have been tempted to speculate that the sender of these masks was targeting you, Detective. However, given that you both had a connection to the dead man and that the first mask had pictures of her," she said, indicating Cindy, "while this mask had pictures of you, I think it's safe to say that you are a group target."

"Truer words have never been spoken," Traci burst out.

Everyone turned to stare at her.

"What are you suggesting by your statement?" Lorraine asked.

"What happens to one of us happens to all of us," Traci said. "We're all connected."

~

We're all connected, Cindy thought as she stared hard at Traci. Even Matthews? Are you related to him? Are you working with him against us?

It seemed absurd. After all, Traci had been married to Mark for a long time, well before they all got on Matthews' radar. Then again, Mark and Paul had been partners. Before that they'd worked for the same police department. It was conceivable that Matthews would have wanted someone close to monitor his son.

Just like the old lady at the nursing home was watching his grandson.

A shudder passed over her. She didn't like the thoughts that she was thinking. Jeremiah was right, this could well be a ruse to get them to suspect her, and, in turn, each other. Divide and conquer was how the saying went. She wished the detectives would get out of there so they could talk to Traci, show her the phone, and figure this out together.

She blinked, remembering what they had been discussing just moments before. Tanner, or rather, Felix was dead.

"When did Felix die?" she asked.

"Two days ago. He appears to have had a head-on collision with a tree."

They all glanced uneasily at each other.

"I didn't realize he was out of prison yet," Cindy said.

"He was afforded a minimum sentence in exchange for testimony against other parties, and was out on parole is my understanding," Lorraine said. "The accident happened about forty-five miles outside of Pine Springs on a fairly isolated stretch of road. There were no witnesses."

"How on earth did this psycho get hold of Felix's face in time to send it to us earlier today?" Mark asked.

"I'm assuming he didn't harvest the skin himself which would suggest an accomplice."

"How about the police reports, the coroner's reports? Was his face intact at the accident scene? Was it removed at the coroner's just like the guard today?"

Cindy barely heard Mark's questions because her mind was busy thinking about where Felix had been killed. A terrible suspicion gripped Cindy.

"You said the accident happened on an isolated road about forty-five miles outside of Pine Springs?"

"Yes, why?"

"Which direction?"

Lorraine frowned. "I believe it was east. It was out away from civilization. Doesn't seem to be much of interest in that area."

"Yes, there is," Cindy said.

She locked eyes with Jeremiah who nodded slowly. Out of the corner of her eye she could see Geanie start as she, too, realized the implications of that.

"What is it?" Lorraine asked.

"I believe he was heading to Green Pastures."

Mark groaned. "Of course he was," he said, his voice haunted.

His hands were shaking and he looked like he had just seen a ghost. As Cindy glanced around the room, she realized they all looked that way, except for Jeremiah who was wearing his mask of inscrutability.

"Explain the significance of this to me," Lorraine said.

Cindy just stared at Mark for a moment. She didn't know how much the two New Orleans detectives already knew or how much they should let them know. They could be working for Matthews, after all.

Mark cleared his throat. "The man who is sending us these masks, who we believe attacked Gerald Wilson and put him in the coma, had an adult son who was killed three years ago at this campsite area called Green Pastures."

"I see. Why do you think Felix Hoskins was going there?"

"Felix was a reporter," Mark said. "Maybe he was doing a follow-up on the story."

"Why? Was he connected to the original story?"

Mark looked at Cindy and she shrugged. She had no idea if Felix had even reported on the horrors that had happened at Green Pastures although it was certainly possible. One or more reporters at his newspaper would have. Beyond that she had no idea what possible connection Felix could have had to the cult, the attempted massacre of the campers, or Not Paul.

"I don't know, but I can find out," Mark said wearily.

He looked exhausted, broken almost. The Not Paul drama just kept coming years later and every time it seemed that they were almost finished with it something new always sprang up.

"Mark, are you okay?" Cindy asked softly.

"I just want this nightmare to be over," he admitted.

"Then help us help you," Lorraine said.

He looked up at her. "Lady, I gotta be honest. At this point I don't know who to trust. No, I take that back. I trust the five people that are here with me. Anyone else is suspect as far as I'm concerned."

Cindy was surprised that Mark admitted that. It showed just how done he was with the whole situation. She also worried for him since she was no longer entirely sure that everyone in their group could be trusted.

Lorraine sat down on the edge of the chair facing Mark and then stared intently at him.

"I understand," she said softly. "I've been there, too."

Mark rubbed his eyes and Lorraine did, too.

"It's hard to know who to trust, especially when you've been betrayed by someone close to you," he said.

"I know. I was betrayed once and it changed me, made me see the world differently," she said, her voice soft.

Mark leaned forward and so did she.

Cindy noticed that the way Lorraine was sitting was an exact mirror of how Mark was sitting. Every time he moved, she moved, too. Cindy had heard about the mirroring technique to gain trust and get people to do what you wanted them to do, but she'd never seen it actually put in practice. At least, not that she was aware of.

A sense of outrage swept through her. She stepped forward and clapped her hands in between them.

Mark straightened abruptly.

"Mark, she's mirroring you, trying to win your trust," Cindy said.

Lorraine sighed and stood up.

"I'm not the enemy," Lorraine said. "In fact, I might be the only person who can help you out of this predicament. I can't offer solutions, though, if I'm unequipped with all the pertinent facts."

"We've told you everything we can," Jeremiah said calmly. "The truth is, we're just as in the dark about everything that's happening as you are."

Lorraine stared at him for a moment with narrowed eyes, obviously trying to read him.

"I sincerely doubt it," she said at last.

~

Detective Lewis was smart, Jeremiah would give her that. He'd watched as she tried to soften up Mark and he was grateful that Cindy had stepped in before he'd needed to.

Mark was exhausted mentally more than physically. This whole problem had been weighing on his mind for too long. He needed an end to the uncertainty, an end to the puzzle, and most certainly an end to the threat of Matthews.

He hadn't realized that Felix was out of prison. Normally he should have been paying closer attention to things like that. In Felix's case, though, Jeremiah hadn't thought of him as any kind of threat to the six of them.

But clearly Matthews thought he was a threat.

Jeremiah wondered exactly what it was that tied Felix to this whole mess. If he had actually been heading to Green Pastures, which was still officially closed, then he must have had a reason.

Maybe he was looking for something, but what physical evidence could remain at the camp that he'd be interested in? Why was he pursuing a story related to it at all? After all, Green Pastures was old news.

I wonder if he discovered something new? Jeremiah thought.

There was something very wrong with all of it. How would Matthews have even known about Felix and his trip to potentially explore Green Pastures? What could have alerted Matthews and what could Felix have potentially found that was a threat?

They needed to talk to the people Felix interacted with and find out if they had any idea what he'd been working on or why he'd tried to visit the campsite.

When the detective had said whose face the mask had been, his initial thought was that it was because Felix was connected to Cindy. That had seemed odd, though, given that it was such a tenuous connection at best. If he just wanted to kill and use someone she knew to terrorize her, there were so many other potential victims, particularly a friend or coworker from the church, that would have made a better target.

Then the Green Pastures connection came to light and shifted his thinking. There was too much they didn't know about all the players. It felt like trying to put together a puzzle without having a picture to go on while missing a third of the pieces.

It was no wonder Mark was starting to crumble.

The detectives finished up with them for the moment and left to go downstairs and question room service staff and the poor bellboy whose job it had been to deliver the ice bucket.

Jeremiah didn't think they'd find anything of interest.

"Food's getting cold, or probably is cold," Geanie said after the detectives left.

Jeremiah no longer felt much like eating. Then he remembered that the restaurant had been Traci's suggestion, taking them someplace other than their intended food destination.

He shared a look with Cindy and could see that she was also wrestling with what to do about that in light of their earlier discovery.

"I don't think this day can get any more messed up," Mark said.

A moment later Traci's burner phone that was inside Jeremiah's pocket began to ring.

10

"Be careful when you say things like that," Cindy said sarcastically to Mark.

"Why?" he asked.

"Things can always get more messed up," Jeremiah said, pulling the phone slowly from his pocket.

He watched Traci for signs of recognition on her part.

"Put it on speakerphone," he said as he handed it to Cindy.

She took the phone and did as he instructed.

"Yes," she said briefly.

"I imagine they've found my latest gift," a deep male voice said.

Mark started up from the chair, his face devoid of color. Jeremiah could tell that the detective recognized the voice. This had to be Matthews.

"Uh huh," Cindy said.

"Keep up the good work. I'll be in touch soon."

The caller hung up.

"That was Matthews! How was he calling your phone?" Mark asked.

Jeremiah shook his head slowly, eyes still glued to Traci.

"It's not my phone. We found it when searching the luggage for trackers. It was in Traci's bag."

Mark blinked several times then turned to stare at his wife.

"You have a burner phone?" he asked.

"It's not mine. I've never seen it before!" Traci exclaimed.

"Matthews was clearly expecting a woman to answer that call," Geanie said quietly.

"Well, there are two other women here," Traci said, glaring first at her then at Cindy.

"Only one of us has the maiden name Matthews," Cindy said quietly.

"What is happening?" Mark demanded.

"You're all crazy!" Traci said. "Mark! Tell them."

Mark was staring, slack-jawed.

"Mark!" Traci snapped.

"She's my wife. We love each other. We have children together. She couldn't possibly be involved with that man," he finally managed to stammer.

"Mark, who did you meet first? Paul or Traci?" Cindy asked.

"I don't know."

"How do you not know?" Geanie asked.

"I met them both at roughly the same time, but that doesn't prove anything."

"You know me. You know my whole family. Do you honestly think I'm capable of being in league with that monster?" Traci demanded, looking around.

Jeremiah held up his hand before anyone could answer. This was about to get ugly, and he needed to put a stop to it.

"Let's all just settle down," he said.

All of the others turned to glare at him.

"After all, there's only one of us that's lied to all the others, who's trained in subterfuge and spying, and all of it. Why don't we ask Jeremiah why he planted that phone in my bag?" Traci demanded.

"He didn't, I was the one who found the phone in your bag," Cindy said, coming to his defense.

"Yeah, but who chose which bags you each searched?"

"Jeremiah did. He didn't want to paw through women's underwear," Cindy said.

"So, he had plenty of time all day to plant it in my bag and let you conveniently find it. After all, if you're looking for a liar and a killer you only have to look to him," Traci said.

Jeremiah cleared his throat loudly.

"As the group's resident obfuscator, spy, and killer I can tell you that this kind of distrust and fear is exactly what Matthews wants. That's why he planted the phone in Traci's luggage for us to find."

"Yes, Jeremiah and I discussed that when we found it, how this could be a trick of Matthews'," Cindy said grudgingly.

"We're all tired. We're all hungry. We need to eat something and get some rest," Jeremiah said. "Then tomorrow we'll figure out how to take this monster down so he can't hurt anyone again."

Stony silence greeted him, so he turned toward Cindy, his eyes appealing to her. Cindy bit her lip and looked away.

"Cindy," he said softly.

She walked over and hugged Traci.

"I'm sorry I jumped to conclusions. I'm tired and scared, but that's no excuse. Honestly, I didn't think you could be involved, but the conversation with Matthews spooked me."

"Do you think he knew how we'd react to that if it sounded like he was actually trying to talk to a collaborator?" Joseph asked.

"He's smart enough," Jeremiah said. "And it was incredibly effective."

"I'm sorry, Traci," Geanie said sheepishly.

"Me, too," Traci said, looking at all of them in turn.

"How about we eat our cold Chinese food and then get some sleep," Jeremiah suggested.

They sat down at the table and divvied up the Chinese food. Jeremiah watched carefully and noted that there were only three of the eight entrees that Traci was eating from. He ate from the same ones even though he put a small portion of food from a fourth on his plate. He left that one alone, only eating what she ate. This way it wasn't as noticeable what he was doing.

He wished he could signal to Cindy what he was doing, but there was no way he could manage it without drawing suspicion. It worried him, but he reasoned that if the food had been tampered with it wouldn't actually be deadly. After all, Matthews was just getting started and it was clear he at least wanted Cindy and Mark alive to play the game with him.

"You know, I'm even more tired than I thought," Joseph admitted, the first to speak once they started eating. "The fact that my body is still on California time isn't even helping."

"It's been a very long, very full day," Jeremiah said. "I should think we'll all sleep pretty hard tonight."

"I hope so," Mark said, his face pale and drawn.

"I think we need to seriously look at beefing up Gerald's security or getting him out of there," Cindy said contemplatively.

"I'm not sure he's going to be in any more danger now that Matthews has us here and has our attention," Jeremiah said.

"I'd feel better if we did something," Cindy said.

The others nodded.

"We'll discuss it in the morning," Jeremiah said firmly.

They were all too tired to make good decisions. He knew from experience that it was time to take a break and get some rest before things became worse.

After they finished eating, Cindy and Jeremiah said goodnight to the others and headed to their room across the hall. Jeremiah was relieved that the strand of Cindy's hair he'd put in the lock was still in place.

They made it into the room and Jeremiah secured the door behind them. Cindy moved through the living area to the bedroom and sat down on her bed. She stared off into space.

He waited for her to say something, but she seemed lost in thought. He grabbed his stuff and headed to the bathroom to get ready for bed. When he came back a few minutes later she was still sitting there.

"You okay?" he asked.

She turned, looked at him, and then smirked.

"Nice pajamas," she said.

He was wearing a pair of pajamas she had given him for Christmas that were covered in cats holding hearts. He'd been surprised to discover that they were indeed guy's pajamas.

"Thanks. I hope you like them," he said.

"What I like is that you're wearing them. Most guys wouldn't have."

"Well, in case you hadn't noticed, I'm not most guys."

"Actually, I had noticed that," she said as she stood up and walked over to him.

"Glad to hear it."

She gave him a lingering hug that he found more than a little distracting. Then she grabbed her stuff and headed into the bathroom.

When she emerged a few minutes later she was wearing a knee-length nightgown that matched his pajamas.

"That's adorable."

She smirked. "Since I'm getting married in a few months I figured I should start upgrading my sleepwear."

"Really?"

"Yup. You should see some of the things I bought last week."

"I'd like to," he said.

"If you're a very good boy, you will."

"When?"

"Oh, I'd say a little under eleven months."

"An eternity," he said with a sigh.

"I promise you, totally worth the wait," she said with an impish smile.

"I'm going to hold you to that."

She gave him a quick kiss then got into her bed, sliding under the covers. He turned off the light and then retreated to his bed.

"You know…" she said, her voice thoughtful.

"Yes?" he asked, thinking she was ready to talk about everything that had happened that day.

"I also bought some new bras and underwear."

"You're trying to kill me, aren't you?"

"I've got them in a special suitcase where I'm putting honeymoon stuff."

"And where do you keep this special suitcase?" he asked, happy to continue flirting.

"I'm not telling. And don't you dare go looking."

"Uh huh, sure."

"I'm serious. I'll tell you what my parents always told us when we were kids, and we knew there were birthday or Christmas presents in the house."

"And what is that?"

"If you find them and see them, I will know and I will return everything I bought."

"So mean."

"No, just prefer to be able to see the look on your face when you open your presents."

"You're my present," he said.

"Exactly."

He didn't have to see her face to know that she was smirking again. It was there in her voice. He loved that she was able to talk and think about something lighthearted when they were in the middle of death and horror. It was a coping mechanism, but it also showed just how far she'd come since they'd met. She had grown a lot as a person. He hoped that he had, too. He believed it to be true, and he owed it all to her.

"Penny for your thoughts?" she said.

"I'm imagining unwrapping my present very, very slowly," he said teasingly.

There was a pause and then she asked, "Do you think red and green are too cliché?"

"For what?" he asked, struggling to follow the change in the thread of conversation.

"For wedding colors."

"I think you should pick whatever you want."

"But do you think it's okay that I want the obvious Christmas colors?"

"I think it's fine. Whatever makes you happy is great with me."

"What colors would you pick?"

"I don't know," he said. "What colors go with eloping this weekend?"

"You're impossible."

"No, just really focused on the end result. I want to be married. Whatever decorations or trappings or rituals you want to add to that are just fine with me."

She sighed in obvious frustration.

"I think red and green are very pretty together. There's a reason they pair well," he said, hoping that appeased her.

"What do you think Matthews' end game is?" she asked, jumping track again.

"I really wish I knew. Most men, even killers and terrorists, it's fairly easy to understand what they want and what they're trying to accomplish. Matthews is smart, but he doesn't think like other people do. He's got some kind of mental illness and it makes him unpredictable. I'm sure to him his plans and schemes are incredibly logical and well laid out, but until I can understand him better, I can't anticipate what he'll do next or what he wants to accomplish or even why he's doing all this."

"That's frustrating," she said.

"Tell me about it. I'm not used to feeling like I'm not only ten steps behind but also like I have no idea what path we're even on."

"What I can't figure out is why he's even bothering with us. I mean, it's not like we are any actual threat to him," she said. "And if this is some kind of warped revenge for the fact that his son is dead, well, he's about three years late by my calculations."

"I agree. Maybe we've just gotten onto his radar and we're an interesting challenge, playthings he can manipulate and torture. Or maybe he's eliminating everyone who had contact with his son."

"In that case, why not kill his grandson? Why have that old lady keep such a strict watch on him?" Cindy asked.

"Excellent questions. Something tells me that Matthews has no intention to live out the rest of his life in quiet and anonymity. He's got to be planning something."

"And he sees us as a threat?"

"Something like that," Jeremiah said.

A chilling voice suddenly boomed in the darkness. "On the contrary, I see you as entertainment."

11

Cindy sat straight up with a scream.

She heard a thud and a moment later light flared on in the room. Jeremiah stood by the light switch, looking wildly around.

The evil voice chuckled.

“Having a problem seeing me, my dear?” he asked.

Her heart was pounding so hard she could actually hear it. Blood was roaring in her ears, and she clutched at the covers even as she strained to figure out where the voice was coming from.

Jeremiah prowled around the room, eyes roving everywhere.

“I thought it very touching, hearing you talk about your upcoming nuptials. I hope that I’m invited.”

“You are not!” Cindy shouted.

“That’s a pity. I guess I’ll just have to crash it then. That is, if you both live long enough. Honestly, long engagements tempt fate, you know. It’s almost like you’re waiting for something terrible to happen to one of you in the meantime.”

“You stay away from us and stay away from our wedding,” Cindy said, her voice shaking.

Jeremiah had moved to the nightstand next to his bed.

"It's a little late for that, my dear. After all, we've been dancing together for so long now, even if you didn't know it was me you were dancing with."

Jeremiah picked the burner phone up off the nightstand. The voice was coming from it, but much louder than even if it had been on speakerphone. Jeremiah turned it over in his hand, inspecting it.

"Did your son run away from you or did you send him to replace the boy, Paul, that you kidnapped?" Cindy asked.

"So many questions you have and that's the one you ask?"

"You've got a better one?" she asked.

"Dozens, starting with 'Where am I'?"

"Where are you?"

"That would be telling. Besides, I know how much you enjoy the hunt. I'd never deprive you of that."

"You don't know anything about me," Cindy hissed.

"Oh, sweet child, I know so much more about you than you'll ever know about me."

"What do you want?"

There was another chuckle. "To officially welcome you to my city. Let the games begin."

Jeremiah pulled the battery out of the phone and dropped both on his bed. Cindy leapt out of hers, flew to him, and threw her arms around him.

She started crying and Jeremiah stroked her back. The voice in the darkness had terrified her more than anything had in a long, long time.

"He's a monster!" she said in between sobs.

"Yes, he is. And I'm going to kill him," Jeremiah said, his voice hard.

"What if he kills you first?" she asked, shuddering at the thought. Matthews had likely killed the people whose faces he had turned into masks. The man was capable of anything.

"A lot better than him have tried and failed. Besides, I don't think he wants us dead. At least, not yet."

~

Jeremiah was doing his best to comfort Cindy, but it was hard given how rattled he was. Matthews was a psychopath, but he was incredibly cunning. Jeremiah had slipped up in not checking the phone more thoroughly. They were lucky it had just been a radio and not a bomb.

A couple minutes later Cindy stopped crying. She pulled away from him and wiped her eyes.

"I got your shirt all wet," she said.

He wanted to say something cute or clever, but he just couldn't come up with anything.

"It's fine."

"Should we wake the others?"

He hesitated then shook his head. "Let's wait and tell them in the morning. Keeping us on edge and sleep deprived could be part of his plan. We can't all be awake all night."

"But you're going to be?" she asked.

"Do you want me to be?"

"Yes and no," she admitted.

"I understand."

They talked for about another half hour before Cindy was calm enough to go back to bed. For himself, he decided to stay up and keep watch for a while although he believed there would be no more surprises that night.

~

Cindy didn't know whether it was the jet lag, the time zone difference, or exhaustion from stress, but when she finally woke up it was nearly ten. She sat up and saw Jeremiah sitting in a chair, dressed.

"Good morning," he said with a smile.

"Did you sleep at all?" she asked, barely covering a yawn.

"I slept enough."

"Have you talked to anyone else yet?"

"Mark texted about ten minutes ago that everyone over there just woke up."

"At least I'm not alone," she said.

She got up, took a quick shower, and got dressed. As soon as she was ready, they headed across the hall to the other room. Geanie, Joseph, and Mark were in the sitting room.

"Traci's just finishing up," Mark said.

They told the others what had happened.

"You must have been terrified," Geanie said. "Having that voice just come out of the darkness."

"It was pretty awful," Cindy admitted.

"That would have given me nightmares," Traci said, having come out into the room in time to hear most of the story.

Cindy shook her head ruefully. "I had nightmares, but not about that."

"About what then?"

“I dreamed I was in a bridal shop looking at all these bridesmaid dresses and the sales lady kept screaming at me that I just had to choose.”

“Dresses?” Traci asked.

“Actually colors,” Cindy said. “I finally pointed to the red and green ones.”

“Then I think you know what you really want,” Geanie said.

“But then I said I’d take the silver and gold ones.”

“Second guessing yourself. I still think you want the red and green.”

“Is it too cliché?” Cindy asked.

“What?” Mark asked, looking confused.

“Red and green for a Christmas wedding?”

“It’s not cliché. It’s practically a requirement,” Geanie said. “Besides, you know I look awesome in red.”

Cindy rolled her eyes.

“Do the colors make you happy?” Joseph asked.

“Yes,” Cindy said.

“Then that’s what matters,” he said.

“I guess.”

“What does Jeremiah think?”

“He doesn’t have an opinion. He says that a lot.” Cindy couldn’t keep the frustration out of her voice as she glanced at him.

“And that’s a bad thing?” Geanie guessed.

“Of course it is. The groom’s job is to give an opinion when asked, even if it’s the bride’s opinion and he’s just parroting it back,” Joseph said with a smile.

Geanie actually made a snorting sound in his direction. “Says the guy who had his own opinions on everything.”

It wasn't exactly the most appropriate time to be discussing the wedding colors, but it was helping her feel like there was something real and tangible she could hold onto. It reminded her that there was a future beyond this moment, this city, this psychopath.

~

Mark's phone rang and he looked at it. "It's the detectives," he said.

He stood up, meaning to take it in the other room, but then remembered that the people around him were his friends and fellow victims. This was information they needed, too.

"What did you find?" he asked.

"Good morning to you as well," Lorraine said smoothly. "I trust that your slumber went undisturbed."

Mark debated whether or not to tell her about the phone. He decided to hold off for the moment.

"I've had better," he said.

That much was certainly true, even if he hadn't been the one who had to deal with Matthews the night before.

"I'm chagrined to hear that."

"I'm chagrined, too," he said, trying to keep the sarcasm out of his voice. He just wanted to get the pleasantries out of the way and figure out why she was calling.

"We did hear back from the laboratory, and I wanted to share the findings with you," she said.

Finally, progress, he thought.

"It was a bit…unexpected."

"What was it?" Mark asked.

"We got a match on the DNA for the second mask," she said.

~

Cindy watched as the all the color left Mark's face. He sat down abruptly.

"Okay, thanks for calling," he whispered.

As he buried his face in his hands, the phone slipped from his fingers and hit the floor. Cindy quickly stepped forward and picked it up. She carefully placed the phone next to Mark then stepped back.

The look on his face and the fact that he still wasn't speaking scared her. She glanced at Traci who looked just as frightened as Cindy felt. Traci sat down gingerly next to Mark and started rubbing his back.

"What is it?" she asked, voice low.

He looked up and tears were running down his cheeks. She mentally braced herself for whatever news he was about to deliver.

"They figured out…the second mask…whose skin it is…was," Mark said slowly.

Cindy looked around at the others. They all looked as scared as she felt.

"It's someone we knew?" Traci asked softly.

Mark nodded his head.

"Whose face was it?" Jeremiah asked.

A shudder passed through Mark. He looked like he was trying to speak but was having trouble getting the words to come out. He kept opening and closing his mouth and shaking his head.

He took a deep breath, grabbed Traci's hand that was on his shoulder, and whispered.

"Not Paul."

12

Everyone gasped in shock.

"How is that even possible?" Traci blurted out moments later. "He's been dead for years."

"Nearly three," Jeremiah said softly, remembering watching the man die when he was shot at Green Pastures and then having to bury him in a shallow grave. The body had been recovered later and reinterred in a cemetery. "And his head was destroyed by the bullet that hit it so there wouldn't have been a face to take."

"I don't know," Mark muttered. "The detective said that the skin had been aged."

"So it was probably taken either shortly before or after his second burial," Jeremiah said softly.

"And he could have made a mask from a different part of the skin, I guess," Geanie said slowly.

"Why would Matthews have done that?" Cindy asked with a shudder.

"He couldn't have wanted a keepsake of his son," Geanie said, looking like she might be sick.

"Mark made fun of me for having Rachel and Ryan's baby shoes bronzed," Traci said. "I can't even imagine…who would want something like that?"

"Maybe he collects them, like trophies. We all assumed that the one sent to Cindy yesterday was the first, but clearly it wasn't," Jeremiah said grimly.

"Why would someone do that?" Joseph asked, echoing Cindy's earlier question.

"Serial killers often collect things from their victims," Mark said.

"And while we've thought of Matthews as a cult leader, kidnapper, and potential mass murderer, we hadn't really thought of him in that light," Jeremiah said.

"Another serial killer," Cindy whispered.

Jeremiah put his hand on her back to steady her. He could tell from the look on her face that she was having flashbacks to her own experiences with the Passion Week Killer. She looked up at him, her eyes a little glassy.

"How do I get so lucky?" she asked.

"You mean how do we get so lucky," Joseph said grimly. "It impacted us all."

"I can't believe he'd do that to his own son," Mark said, tears starting anew. "I think of Ryan-" He broke off, unable to go on.

"It's okay, Mark," Jeremiah said softly, his heart going out to the other man. They were all in shock, all in pain, but Mark was the one who was most deeply affected. "We will find him, and we will stop him."

"How? This is his town," Geanie said. "That's what he told us and that's what we've seen. He's got this place wired. Who knows how many people are working for him?"

Jeremiah could hear the despair in her voice and it wasn't good, particularly not from Geanie. He was used to her being optimistic, often painfully so. She had grown darker of late, but this was a look he didn't like on her.

"By taking advantage of that," he said.

They all turned to look at him, their expressions telling him very clearly that they thought he was crazy.

He smiled. “The home advantage does give an adversary the upper hand. However, there is a tendency to get lazy, complacent, and to start making sloppy mistakes because one feels too secure in their own home, their own city. So, we need to set our own traps while he’s busy not paying attention.”

“Sounds good in theory. How do we put it into practice?” Joseph asked.

“It will take some time, some ingenuity, and some money,” Jeremiah warned.

“This is my top priority right now. I’ll give whatever time it takes,” Traci said.

“You’ve got all my creativity at your disposal,” Geanie told him.

“And, obviously, I’m happy to pay,” Joseph said.

Mark and Cindy just stood there, looking around at all the rest of them. They were both still in shock, but they were the most important pieces of the puzzle. Fortunately, there was a lot that the rest of them could accomplish while Mark and Cindy pulled themselves back together.

“Then let’s get this done,” Jeremiah said.

“What do we do first?” Geanie asked.

“Get something to eat. We all missed breakfast. Let’s go get some lunch.”

“Do we need to take a dozen different taxis to get there?”

“No. If he wants to have us followed, let him,” Jeremiah said.

~

The last thing Cindy felt like doing was eating. She understood, though, that it was necessary to keep her strength up. She was shaken by what they had discovered, and she couldn't understand Matthews' sick, warped idea of a game.

More than that, something he'd said in the middle of the night kept playing over and over in her mind.

After all, we've been dancing together for so long now, even if you didn't know it was me you were dancing with.

What did he mean by that?

She kept telling herself it was just something creepy he'd said to get inside her head and freak her out. He was trying to take more power than he actually had and make her afraid. Deep down, though, she didn't believe it. There had been the ring of truth in his voice when he said it.

She was so fixated on thinking about it that she hadn't realized that Geanie had ordered a gigantic tray of beignets until the waiter set them down on the table. They looked and smelled amazing and far more appealing than the seafood dish that Cindy had ordered. She found herself digging into the beignets and ignoring her own meal.

"What do you need?" Joseph asked as he started in on his food.

"For starters, I need a hacker," Jeremiah said.

"I know a couple of computer guys, but they can get squirrely sometimes. I'm not sure I'd be comfortable asking them to do anything illegal," Joseph said.

"That's okay, I know where I can find one," Jeremiah said. "Give me a couple of minutes."

He stood up.

"Where are you going?" Cindy asked, feeling herself start to panic.

"It's okay. I'm going to make a phone call. It will take a few minutes, but I'll be back."

Traci reached over and grabbed her hand.

"Let him do what he has to do," she urged.

Anxiety was flooding Cindy. She had no desire to stop Jeremiah. She just really, really wished she was going with him.

~

Jeremiah walked outside and headed down the street. He made fifteen turns and doubled back twice to make sure no one was following him. Then he made his way into an office building where everyone seemed to be out to lunch. He walked past reception and found an empty office. He sat down and dialed a number from memory. He just hoped that Martin, the C.I.A. officer, was able to pick up.

The phone rang twice and then he heard a familiar voice.

"Who is this?" the spy answered, voice tense.

"It's your Jewish cousin calling," Jeremiah said.

There was a pause and then Martin said, "I hope you're calling to get my address for the wedding invitation."

"Not so much."

"Not in a good place at the moment," Martin said.

Two shots rang out in rapid succession.

"Glad you took the call."

"What is it you need?" Martin asked.

There was a rapid series of shots.

"A hacker, a good one. I need a worm created."

"Don't tell me what you want her for," Martin hissed.

"Do you have someone?"

"Yeah."

The sound of automatic gunfire erupted, louder than the earlier shots.

"I'll text you a number."

"I need it sent secured."

"Fine. I'll handle it shortly…I hope," Martin added as there was another volley of gunfire.

The spy grunted suddenly.

"You hit?" Jeremiah asked.

"Grazed. Anything else?"

"Yeah, your address for the wedding invitation. We're not mailing them out for a few months still, but who knows when I'll talk to you next."

There was a snort on the other end of the line. "We're in the process of moving. I'll have someone reach out to you and get you something you can use. Gotta run."

The call ended and Jeremiah hung up. He said a silent prayer for Martin's safety during the fight. He then made a quick call to another number in the building so if the owner of the office hit the redial button on his phone he wouldn't reach the spy.

Jeremiah got up and walked out of the office. As he hit the lobby several people were starting to stream into the building and he gave each a glance, checking for familiar faces. There were none.

He exited and headed back to the café where he'd left everyone. When he got there, he noticed that all three ladies had managed to get powdered sugar all over their clothes. Each of them, though, looked in much better spirits than they had before. They were also clearly relieved to see him.

"Well?" Joseph asked.

"Should have a name in a few minutes. Hopefully."

There was no text from Martin by the time he finished eating about half an hour later. He really hoped the other man was okay. He was getting impatient, though. The longer they delayed the more opportunity Matthews had to strike at them again.

"What do you need the hacker for?" Joseph asked when he saw Jeremiah check his phone for the tenth time.

Jeremiah leaned in and lowered his voice.

"I need someone to create a worm to search for any connections between anyone we know and New Orleans," he said.

Joseph frowned. "You don't need a hacker for that. The code already exists. You just need someone to grab it off the dark web and run it."

"Computers was not my area of expertise. I wouldn't want to mess up and get us caught," Jeremiah said.

Joseph stood abruptly, dropped a couple of hundred dollar bills on the table and walked toward the front of the restaurant. Surprised, everyone else scrambled to catch up with him. Jeremiah trailed behind, keeping a wary eye on the other diners and the waitstaff. No one seemed to be paying attention to them. Neither was there anyone who looked like they were trying to avoid paying attention to them.

Joseph hailed a minivan cab and they all piled in.

"Where to?" the driver asked.

"The nearest place to buy a computer," Joseph said.

"I have my laptop with me," Geanie said.

"That won't cut it," Joseph said shortly.

Twenty minutes later the driver had dropped them off at a big box store. Joseph told the rest of them to wait in the van. He went into the store and emerged a few minutes later with a large computer box that the driver helped him put in the back.

From there they headed back to the hotel. Joseph set up the computer and logged onto the hotel's wifi.

"It would be better with a direct connection, faster, but this will get the job done," he said.

A couple of minutes later he leaned back in his chair and looked at the rest of them.

"What on earth are you doing and how did you learn to do it?" Traci asked, wide-eyed.

"The worm to find and collate all that information is easy to acquire if you know where to look," Joseph said. "It's actually a very straightforward code, just a couple hundred lines. What's harder is the other part of it, the memory management part which is what keeps it from being found. You don't want the machines that you're going to be impacting to know it's there. The irony is, those machines are doing most of the work, they just can't know it."

"How long will this take?" Jeremiah asked.

"It depends on the total number of machines and the connection. With a thousand machines and a wired connection it would take ten to fifteen minutes to retrieve all the information, collate it, and make it something useful. Ten thousand machines would take half an hour or more. Since we're on wifi, it will take a bit longer."

"Why couldn't you use my laptop?" Geanie asked.

"The code is too tightly written. Your laptop would start to superheat and the battery would drain. Plus, it really doesn't have enough memory, which we should change. To do this you really need a computer with a one terabyte drive and lots of memory."

"I didn't realize that you knew this kind of stuff," Traci said.

"Join the club," Geanie muttered as she stared at her husband.

~

Mark still wasn't exactly sure what Jeremiah and Joseph were hoping to accomplish. He was still in shock or he might have tried harder to figure it out. Instead, he decided to focus on what he could do.

He moved into the bedroom while the others were in the sitting room. He sat down heavily on his and Traci's bed and then called Harry, the coroner back in Pine Springs. He explained what was going on and the other man listened quietly.

"Do you have a picture of the mask?" Harry asked when Mark had finished.

"Yes. I'm sending it to your email right now."

Mark sent a picture of the mask which he had taken before the other detectives had arrived.

"Give me a sec," Harry said.

Mark waited while the coroner took a look at the picture.

"You're sure the skin belonged to your former partner, Not Paul, as you call him?"

"That's what I'm asking you. The detectives here said the DNA matched."

"Unfortunately, I can't really tell you from looking at this. I can see faint veining which would lead me to believe it might be from somewhere like the forearm, but I just can't be certain. What I can tell you is that when he was buried, the skin on his body was intact. What happened after that, I don't know."

"I need the body exhumed," Mark said.

"That's a tall order."

"I need to be sure that this is him."

"If New Orleans police said it was-"

"I don't know if I can trust them. I'm not sure who all is working with Matthews," Mark said. "Besides, I need to make sure this isn't another bait-and-switch and that we really are dealing with the same guy, my former partner."

"I know what you've been through the last three years," Harry said sympathetically.

"Yeah."

"I know you need closure on this."

"You're not kidding."

"I'm just worried that if you keep going down this road that you might not like what you find," Harry said softly.

"What does that mean?" Mark asked.

There was a long pause and then Harry said, "I'll put in the paperwork to get the ball rolling."

There was a click as Harry hung up. Mark sat for a moment, staring at the phone, wondering what the ominous warning had been about. Could Harry be involved, too?

Mark felt like he was drowning and that he was grasping at straws, just trying to keep his head above water.

He saw movement in the doorway, and he lifted his head. Jeremiah was standing there, a grim look on his face.

"We found what we're looking for?" Mark said.

Jeremiah nodded.

"And?"

"And you better get out here."

13

Cindy looked up as Jeremiah and Mark came into the room. The detective didn't look good. In fact, she was fairly certain she'd never seen him look worse. The whole thing was getting under his skin, and she couldn't blame him. She couldn't even imagine what kind of thoughts were running through his brain since learning that the mask had been made from the skin of his dead partner.

She shuddered. It was all so very macabre and disturbing. Perhaps that was to be expected given where they were and the man they were going up against.

No, not a man, she thought to herself. Matthews is a monster.

Just thinking about him sent a sick feeling spiraling down in her stomach. She still couldn't fathom what kind of disturbed mind could kidnap children, let alone murder them.

"What did you find?" Mark asked in a flat tone. It was the voice of a man who really didn't want to know the answer but felt obligated to ask the question.

Joseph turned in his chair.

"Jordan Casey."

"Who?" Mark frowned, clearly trying to figure out where he might have heard that name before.

"One of the jurors I was sequestered with during that trial last year," Cindy said.

"Oh no, not another one of them," Mark said. "It seemed like all of them were breaking the law in one way or another."

"Not Jordan. At least, not that we knew of," Cindy said. "He told me he was a pop culture blogger."

"He is," Joseph said, indicating the computer screen. "A fairly popular one by the looks of things. He's got quite a few followers."

Cindy moved closer and saw a picture of Jordan at the top of a page. In the picture he was wearing the same Superman shirt he'd been wearing when she first met him.

"What's his connection to New Orleans?" Mark asked.

"Apparently he's here to cover an event for his blog. The Chewbacchus Krewe is having its Carnival parade and ball this weekend."

"Do we believe that?" Mark asked skeptically.

"He does blog about all things pop culture," Cindy said.

"And the Chewbacchus Krewe celebrates Chewbacca from Star Wars for Carnival. It doesn't get much more pop culture than that," Joseph said.

"Still, I don't like the timing," Mark said.

"Neither do I," Jeremiah said softly. "But I was hoping for a connection, someone we could enlist as an ally. Maybe Jordan can be that ally."

"Unless he's already working for our enemy," Geanie voiced what Cindy knew most of them were worrying about.

"Okay, so what do we do about it?" Mark asked. "I mean, in theory we know roughly where he'll be this weekend if he's attending that parade. A lot can happen between now and then, though."

"Fortunately, we don't have to wait. I know where he is right now," Joseph said softly.

He was staring intently at a new page on the computer. Mark squinted.

"Did you just pull up his credit card information?" the detective asked a moment later.

"That would be illegal," Joseph said, exiting the site.

"Where is he?" Jeremiah asked.

"He's staying at a hotel a block away, and he just charged lunch at the adjacent restaurant to his credit card."

Joseph scribbled an address down on a hotel notepad and tore off the top sheet. Jeremiah stepped forward and quickly grabbed it from him.

"Let's move," Jeremiah said, already halfway to the door.

"I'm going to stay here and see if I can find anything or anyone else that might be able to help us," Joseph said.

"How do you know how to do all this?" Geanie asked her husband.

"One of my college roommates had an uncle who invented half the technology we use today. He visited one weekend and it was…educational," Joseph said, eyes glued to the screen.

Cindy got up and headed to the door. Anything was better than sitting around the hotel room waiting for someone else to decide her fate.

"You don't have to come," Jeremiah said softly.

"Yes, I do," she told him.

Jeremiah's eyes drifted past her to Mark.

"Mark, keep everyone safe until I get back," he said.

"Okay," Mark said, a note of relief in his voice.

"And if you don't want to know the answers, don't ask Joseph what he's doing," Jeremiah added.

"Understood," Mark said with a short nod.

Jeremiah held the door and Cindy walked out in front of him. He closed it and then put a hand on her back as he steered her toward the stairs.

"No elevator?" she asked.

"Let's just say I'd feel safer with the stairs."

They made it to the stairwell and started down, their footsteps echoing on the concrete.

"That was a nice thing you did for Mark, letting him stay behind without making him feel bad about it," she said after they had descended a floor.

"He wouldn't have been any good to us in his current condition. He needs some time to process. And, in the unlikely event that something does happen while we're gone, he has more fight experience than the rest of you put together."

"Make sense."

Fortunately, they only had to walk down seven flights of stairs. Cindy told herself it could easily have been a lot worse. She was still relieved when she reached the bottom. Enclosed stairways like the one in the hotel always made her feel a bit trapped and claustrophobic.

They walked quickly toward Jordan's hotel. She had to work to keep up with Jeremiah's long strides. The entire time they were walking his head was swiveling around, taking in everything around them with steely eyes. He reminded her of an owl she had once seen when camping with her family. The creature spent several minutes twisting and turning its head effortlessly in search of prey. Then it had fixed its great glowing eyes on her. She remembered how startled and ultimately frightened she had been before it finally flew off on silent wings.

They entered the lobby and Jeremiah started to move toward the registration desk. She tapped him on the shoulder, and he spun toward her.

"There he is," she said, pointing.

Jordan was walking toward the elevators. She could only see his profile, but she recognized him instantly.

"Jordan!" she called.

He stopped and turned with a frown, scanning the lobby to see who had called to him. His eyes finally fell on Cindy. He stared at her for a moment, frowning. Then his face registered surprise tinged with a bit of relief. He waved and then started walking toward them.

"Cindy! What on earth are you and your super scary fiancé doing here?" he asked.

She took a deep breath. "It's a long story, one that I want to share with you."

"Okay… that sounds odd, maybe even a little ominous," he said. "I haven't stepped into another murder, have I? I'm just here for the Carnival celebrations. I got here yesterday, and I haven't seen or heard anything out of the ordinary. Well, not out of the ordinary for New Orleans at Carnival, apparently."

"You're about to," Jeremiah said grimly.

Jordan got a strange look on his face. "I have to admit I'm curious but deeply conflicted. I've done some research on you guys. You heard that old joke about if you see George Kennedy on a plane you should immediately get off?"

"I can't say that I have," Cindy said.

"He's in all those old airplane disaster movies. Never mind. More modern reference, if you see the Avengers show up, the only smart course of action is to get the heck out of Dodge because crazy is about to go down."

"Meaning?" Jeremiah prompted.

"Wherever you two go, murder, mayhem, and chaos follow."

"Let's go talk in your room," Cindy said.

"Okay," Jordan said, looking a little reluctant but also very curious.

~

Jeremiah's gut told him that Jordan was okay, but at this point, they couldn't be too careful. There was too much at stake and their adversary had proven himself to be far more clever than even Jeremiah had given the man credit for. As they followed Jordan to his room, Jeremiah kept his eyes moving, intentionally observing everything and everyone in their path.

The room itself was small, cramped even, with no sitting area and barely enough room for the double bed that was in it.

"Sorry," Jordan said. "We can go to a coffee house or something."

"No, this is fine," Cindy said as she perched on the end of the bed.

"I wanted to get a cooler place to stay, but I waited too long to decide I was coming."

"Why did it take so long?" Jeremiah asked, trying to keep the suspicion from his voice.

"I've been wanting to come for the last two years, but the schedule conflicts with a science fiction convention I normally attend. This year the guests I was hoping to interview canceled three weeks ago, so, here I am."

Jordan looked from Jeremiah to Cindy then back again. "So, are you going to tell me who's dead?"

"A number of people," Cindy said.

"Us, too, if we're not careful," Jeremiah added grimly.

"Great, because that makes me feel loads better," Jordan said, the worry clear in his voice. He furrowed his eyebrows. "Why are you talking to me and how did you even find me?"

"The 'how' can wait. As for the 'why', well, we need your help," Jeremiah said.

"I honestly don't know what I could possibly do that the two of you can't," Jordan said.

"We need more eyes and ears," Cindy said.

Jordan frowned. "You mean spies?"

"More like informants," Jeremiah muttered under his breath.

"Security, our own personal neighborhood watch I guess you could say," Cindy said, forcing a smile.

"I'm super confused," Jordan said.

"How many of your readers would you estimate are here in New Orleans?" Jeremiah asked.

"You mean live here or are here for the festivities?" Jordan asked with a frown.

"Either."

"Wow, I honestly don't know. I'd have to check. I mean, I know I have a couple of thousand readers in this state, but I don't know where in the state they live."

“We’d like you to find out as soon as possible,” Jeremiah said.

Jordan was starting to look less confused and more scared.

“Has one of my followers done something?”

“Not yet, but we’re hoping they will,” Cindy said.

Jordan sat down on the floor, his back to the wall and his knees under his chin. He sighed deeply.

“Maybe you should start from the beginning,” Jordan said. “Once Upon a Time it for me.”

“Once upon a time there was a very bad man who was a cult leader and mass murderer. His name was Matthews,” Cindy began.

~

“I hate waiting like this,” Mark said.

“We all do,” Joseph said, his eyes still glued to the computer monitor.

“At least you’re doing something,” Mark groused. “You’re not just twiddling your thumbs like the rest of us.”

“It might not look like it, but it feels like it,” Joseph said grimly. “Matthews is slippery. I haven’t been able to find out any more about him than we already know.”

“He’s probably going by an alias. After all, we know he’s done that before,” Mark said.

“True. I’ve had a worm looking for possible references to him, including both of the names we know him under, and other names composed of the same letters.”

“Anagrams,” Traci said quietly.

“Yes, exactly.”

"Do you think it will turn up anything?" Geanie asked as she moved up behind her husband and began massaging his shoulders.

"I don't know, but if he used that trick once, let's hope that he's done it again. Obviously, the smart thing to do would be to just create a new name altogether, but I'm not sure he would do that."

"Why not?" Traci asked quickly.

"Because this guy likes himself too much. Even if he can't use his own name, he'd want it to be there, hiding in plain sight, mocking us," Mark said, passing a hand through his hair.

Joseph stiffened suddenly.

"What is it?" Mark asked.

"Something like Howie T. M. Basatt?"

Mark swiftly tried to do the anagram in his head, but quickly gave up. "That's an anagram for Tobi A. Matthews?"

"And Matthew Tobias," Joseph said.

"We might have found him. Where does the name pop up?"

"Somewhere bad," Joseph said, his fingers flying across his keyboard.

"Where?" Mark said, his heart beginning to pound in his chest.

"As a representative for Crescent City Rehab."

Mark shook his head, struggling to make the connection.

"He just checked Gerald out of the hospital two minutes ago."

14

"We have to get down there!" Mark half shouted as he made for the door.

"You'll probably be too late, but go! I'll notify the police and see if I can get more information," Joseph called after him.

"I'm going," Geanie said, bolting out the door after Mark.

"I'm staying!" Traci called.

Mark couldn't hear anything else as the door closed. He ran to the elevator with Geanie beside him.

"You don't have to go," he told her as he pounded the call button for the elevator.

"I've been just as stuck and helpless in that hotel room as you," she said hotly.

He looked at her and noted that she looked even angrier and more frustrated than he felt.

"We should have set a guard on Gerald," he said.

"Isn't that what the cops are supposed to be for?" she asked.

"Back home, maybe. I don't know yet what the cops here are for," he admitted.

The elevator began to open, its doors creaking and moving so slowly that he wanted to scream and shove his body through the opening. Geanie finally pushed in and a moment later he was able to as well. He hit the button for the lobby five times even though he knew it wouldn't make the elevator go any faster. Then he pushed the close doors button and watched in agony as the doors repeated their slow progress but in reverse.

"Come on, come on, come on!"

The doors finally closed and what seemed an eternity later slowly began to open again in the lobby. As soon as he could, Mark forced his way through. A minute later he and Geanie were inside a cab and heading to the hospital.

"We're ignoring all protocol," Geanie said tensely.

"Protocol be hanged. It doesn't matter at all if we lose Gerald."

Geanie pulled several bills out of her pocket and held them up so the cab driver could see them in the rearview mirror.

"There's a five-hundred-dollar bonus in it if you get us there in the next five minutes," Geanie said.

By way of answer the cabbie slammed his foot down on the gas, throwing Geanie and Mark back against their seats. The man swerved into oncoming traffic and then back into their lane, cutting off two cars in the process. Then he drove through a pack of pedestrians crossing in the crosswalk, sending them scrambling to avoid being hit.

"And I thought Liam drove like a half-crazed wheelman for the mob," Mark muttered.

"He does," Geanie said with a grunt as she struggled not to slam into Mark as the cab driver made a near-impossible ninety degree right turn.

"Then what do you call this?" Mark asked.

"Hopefully not an audition for the New Orleans Demolition Derby."

Suddenly the cab came to a screeching halt, throwing Mark and Geanie forward so hard they barely avoided smashing their heads into the glass divider between the front seat and the back seat. Geanie shoved the money through the slit in the divider and was out and running before Mark could recover.

"That sho' is one crazy woman-child," the driver said, his voice admiring. "Life with her must be one wild ride."

"Yes. Thank God I'm not the one who's married to her," Mark said as he opened his own door and staggered out of the car.

His phone rang and he answered.

"I believe they're driving a grey van and they should be just pulling away from the hospital's main entrance," Joseph said.

Mark didn't waste time asking the other man how he'd figured that out. Instead, he sprinted forward, eyes scanning the area.

"Grey van!" he shouted to Geanie.

"There!" she shouted, pointing to a van just exiting onto the road.

Mark spun on his heel and sprinted back to the cab they had just left. He yanked open the door and dove in.

"Back so soon?" the driver asked.

"Follow that van!" Geanie ordered as she got in the other side.

The driver laughed as he floored it and veered out onto the main road. "Best fare ever!"

"We can't let them know we're following them," Mark said.

"Can you keep them from spotting us?" Geanie asked at the same time.

"Relax, chéri. They no see us."

Mark hoped the driver was right. Fortunately, the van was easy to keep track of and the driver was heeding the rules of the road. They didn't have to do anything unpredictable to follow. The cab driver kept them consistently four to five cars behind the van.

Mark could feel the anxiety coming off of Geanie and it did nothing to help his own state of mind. He knew that Gerald was in trouble and that even now they could be torturing or killing him in the back of the van instead of waiting to reach their destination. Short of ramming the van and trying to run them off the road there was nothing that they could do at that moment. The cabbie might be having fun, but Mark was willing to bet he'd draw the line at wrecking his cab.

Of course, I'm sure Geanie would just buy him another.

The monetary loss wouldn't be the only potential problem for the driver, though. They couldn't ask him to do that.

The van made a series of turns. The third one had Mark worried, because he wasn't sure if the driver was still taking his normal route or if he was looking for someone tailing him.

Apparently, their driver was thinking the same thing because he drove right by the last left turn without turning.

"Don't worry, I know a short cut. This way they no suspect us," the driver said.

It was sound tactics, but it just ratcheted Mark's anxiety up another couple of notches. The cab driver finally made two left turns and a minute later the grey van came back into view.

"You see?" the driver asked, clearly pleased with himself.

"Great job," Mark said.

"Any idea where he might be going?" Geanie asked.

"I'm not sure, although they've turned in the direction of the Garden District. More direct ways to get there."

So maybe they are looking for tails, Mark thought. That was the only reason he could think of to take a circuitous route.

"Anyways, we find out when we gets there," the driver said.

~

Cindy watched Jordan intently after they'd finished explaining to him who they were up against. The blogger pushed his hair back from his forehead while letting his breath out slowly.

"Okay, that's all very terrifying. To be honest, my skin is crawling at the thought that Matthews could be watching us right now."

"I completely understand," Cindy said.

Jordan gave a short laugh and shook his head. "No, I really don't think you do. You're made for this kind of thing and I'm really not."

And despite all the insanity around them and the fear that had been eating at her heart for two days, Cindy found herself smiling.

"What's so funny?" Jordan asked.

"I'm really not made for this sort of thing," she said.

He rolled his eyes. "Don't be so modest. You eat danger for breakfast. You're the original Cara Dune to this guy's Mando," he said, nodding at Jeremiah.

"Who?" Jeremiah asked with a frown.

"Mando, the Mandalorian, Star Wars?" Jordan rolled his eyes. "She's Moneypenny to your James Bond."

"Now that reference I did get," Jeremiah said.

Cindy glanced at him, trying not to smirk.

"The truth is that five years ago I could never have imagined even being in a situation like this," she told Jordan.

"Well, you cope with it well."

"Thanks," she said, finding that the compliment actually pleased her.

"So, what exactly is it you want my help with?" Jordan asked.

"Matthews seems to have this town wired," Jeremiah said.

"It sounds like it. That's some hecka creepy stuff, knowing what hotel you would be in and all."

"He either has a bunch of people working for him or he has a handful of people that are much better at networking and playing us than we are at playing them," Cindy said.

Jordan nodded slowly as light dawned in his eyes.

"You want to even the playing field."

"Exactly!" she said.

"I'm not sure I want to volunteer to march into Mordor."

"We're not asking you to fight him," Jeremiah said. "We just need our own network, our own eyes and ears."

"So, we went looking for anyone we might know with connections in New Orleans to counter his connections," Cindy said.

"And you found me."

"And we found you," she said.

"Okay, I think I understand."

“We were looking for just a couple of allies, but you are in a unique position,” Jeremiah said.

“I get it,” Jordan told him. “The world used to be a small place with hometowns and villages. Then it got to be big, anonymous, with all the huge cities. Now, thanks to social media, it’s small once again.”

“That’s what we’re counting on,” Jeremiah told him.

“I’ll do what I can. Although, I’ll be honest, I have a really strong urge to pack my stuff, head to the airport, and fly home.”

“If you do, don’t bother packing your stuff first,” Jeremiah said.

“Oh, thanks, because that makes me feel loads better,” Jordan said sarcastically.

Jeremiah just shrugged.

“We would really appreciate your help,” Cindy told Jordan.

“Okay, I’ll do it on one condition.”

“What’s that?” she asked.

“When this is over, you let me interview you for my blog. I’ll do a piece on the real life Shirley Holmes and her man, Watson.”

From the way Jeremiah narrowed his eyes Cindy could guess that he saw their roles as flipped. It was funny in a way, because she would agree. However, to Jordan, she was the focal point because he had been introduced to her first.

“Agreed,” she said, quickly.

“Awesome, okay, tell me what you need me to do.”

~

Mark's patience was wearing thin. It was beginning to seem like the grey van had the intention to keep driving around indefinitely.

"We going to have us a problem soon," the cab driver finally said. "I've got six miles left before I can go no further."

"Why?" Geanie asked.

"No gas. No go."

Mark swore under his breath. It would be too much to hope for that the van was going to stop that soon.

"Where are we?" Geanie asked.

"Two miles from the hospital where we started."

They are trying to run us in circles, Mark thought. But why? If they knew we were watching them for sure they'd try to shake us. Unless they want us following. But why?

His phone vibrated at the same time Geanie's chirped.

"What is it?" he asked.

"Joseph. He sent a text to the group chat but it's all garbled," she said.

~

Jeremiah was hopeful that Jordan and his network would be of help. He'd thought of having the other man transfer to their hotel so they could keep an eye on him. However, they'd been careful on their way to and from his hotel and there was no reason that the blogger would be on Matthews' radar for him to connect that Jordan was in town. The longer they could keep his involvement quiet, the better it would be for all of them.

They arrived back at their hotel just as a text came in from Joseph.

“This is odd,” Cindy said, staring at the text with a frown.

“What did he say?” Jeremiah asked.

“It’s garbled, like he was pocket texting.”

“What letter does it begin with?” Jeremiah asked, praying he was wrong.

“H. Why?”

Jeremiah bolted forward, sprinting toward the stairwell. He knew all he needed to in that moment. Joseph was in trouble. The “H” was almost certainly his attempt to text “Help” which had been thwarted by someone. He yanked open the door to the stairs and began bounding upward, taking three stairs at a time. It would get him there slightly faster than the elevator. Of course, the trade off was that he was expending a lot more energy. Hopefully he wouldn’t need the reserves he was burning to fight off Joseph’s attacker.

He reached their floor, yanked open the door, and went racing down the hall. Some part of his brain urged him to slow, to be cautious, to see and take in the situation before revealing himself. Another part of him knew that his friend might only have a second or two left and that there was no time for caution. He put on an extra burst of speed as he produced the room key from his pocket. The door was closed but a quick tap with the card against the senser and a quick yank of the handle afforded him quick entry. He made it two steps inside when pain exploded against his temple.

15

Jeremiah staggered under the sudden assault.

Idiot! he thought to himself as he slammed into the wall. He bounced off the wall and swung at the large man who had hit him. The man didn't duck, just took the blow right on the cheekbone. The skin split apart. Blood began to run down his face, but he was unfazed. His eyes were almost uncomprehending as he stared at Jeremiah for a moment before launching another attack.

He flew into motion and Jeremiah barely managed to dodge to the side. The man's fist went through the wall where Jeremiah's head had been. Jeremiah tried to take advantage of the moment, but instead was busy blocking a kick that seemed to come out of nowhere. He moved into the room, needing to get some more space to maneuver.

A series of rapid kicks and blows were aimed at him, only a few of which he was able to deflect or dodge. The other man nearly bit him in the arm at one point, but Jeremiah spun, yanking free at the last moment.

Jeremiah had encountered nearly every martial arts system in the world. This was unlike any of them. The man fought more like a wild animal than a human being. It made him unpredictable and twice as dangerous.

Jeremiah took a step back, trying to put distance between him and the other man, but he ended up slamming his back up against the wall. Jeremiah snarled at the man, using a language he would understand. There was no reason, no understanding in the eyes that met his, just a sort of feral savagery.

He's one of the kidnapped kids, Jeremiah realized.

"I'm going to tell your father that you've been a bad boy," Jeremiah said.

A flicker of something new—fear, perhaps—sparked to life in the man's eyes. He made a whining sound deep in his throat and Jeremiah pushed off the wall and drew himself up to his full height.

"Bad, bad boy!" he said as sternly as possible. "Your father will be very angry with you."

The man backed up, dropping his eyes, and he made little moaning sounds of distress. Jeremiah knew he had to tread carefully. He had the advantage for the moment, but he didn't know how far he could push it, what word might inadvertently snap the other man out of it.

What on earth did Matthews do to him?

Jeremiah could feel pity creeping into his mind. He stubbornly pushed it to the side. Whatever had happened to this man as a child was no doubt a monstrosity. But that was the child. This man before him would kill him in the blink of an eye if he could. For him Jeremiah must not feel any pity, nor show any mercy.

Slowly he raised his arm and pointed toward the door of the hotel. "Go home and wait for your father."

The man glanced to either side, whining again, and looked trapped. Jeremiah held his breath, waiting to see if his gamble worked. The man finally tucked his chin down toward his chest and scurried out of the room.

Jeremiah glanced at Joseph who was clambering off the ground and into the computer chair.

"Traci and I are fine, go!" Joseph said, voice hoarse.

Jeremiah nodded then turned and walked cautiously out the door. He could see the man he had been fighting shuffling down the hallway toward the stairwell. Jeremiah followed quietly, his footfalls all but inaudible on the thick carpet.

The elevator door opened as Jeremiah passed it and he ducked inside. At the rate the other man was walking he probably wouldn't be taking the stairs in too much of a hurry and Jeremiah had less risk of being detected if he didn't have to follow him down. Stairwells echoed badly and it was hard to track someone in them without being seen or heard.

Moments later he exited into the lobby. To his surprise he saw Cindy waiting, hovering near the elevators. Her eyes widened when she saw him.

"I wasn't sure if I would get in the way if I followed you up," she told him.

"You did right to stay down here," he said as he led her farther away from the door to the stairwell.

"What's going on?"

"One of Matthews' followers was attacking Joseph and Traci. The man isn't all there, though. I told him to go home, and he appears to be doing that."

Cindy's eyes lit up.

"So, we should be able to follow him."

"I should be able to follow him," Jeremiah corrected.

"Didn't you once tell me it was easier to follow someone if you could tag team with another person?"

"Another trained person."

Cindy folded her arms over her chest and glared at him. He tried glaring back, but gave up seconds later with a sigh.

“Fine, just do everything I say.”

“Absolutely,” she said with a victorious smile.

Just then the door to the stairwell opened and the man came lumbering out. He didn’t look around; he just moved straight forward toward the exit. The fact that he wasn’t paying attention to his environment would work in Cindy and Jeremiah’s favor.

He had heard Mark talk about some of the kidnapped children whose bodies hadn’t been found or who had been otherwise accounted for. They had already encountered the Colbert girl, now a woman. It made sense that this man was one of those boys. The only name Jeremiah could remember hearing from the missing list was Danny Monroe. He wondered if that was who they were following.

The Roosevelt was in the French Quarter and it was nearly impossible to shut out the sights and sounds as they followed Danny, or whoever he was, through the narrow streets. A couple of blocks away he got on a streetcar. It was with some hesitation that Jeremiah and Cindy finally boarded as well and only after he determined that their quarry was still staring down at his feet and not paying attention to anyone around him.

Cindy and Jeremiah put as many people between themselves and the man as possible while still being in a position to see if he got off the trolley.

“Where do you think he’s heading?” Cindy asked softly.

“This line runs to the Garden District. Wouldn’t surprise me if the man we were looking for had a place there,” Jeremiah answered, his voice the merest whisper.

~

Every time the streetcar came to a stop Cindy could feel her heart begin to pound. She kept expecting to be seen by the man they were following. Truth be told, she had no idea if he knew what she looked like, but he would certainly recognize Jeremiah if he laid eyes on him.

Part of her admitted that there was something thrilling in trailing a bad guy, particularly at such close range. The rest of her, though, was fretful. Her thoughts had turned darker than was normal. She kept looking around at the other passengers on the trolly and wondering how many of them might be killed if their quarry were to recognize Jeremiah or her.

It's not like there aren't cemeteries everywhere.

She shook her head violently, upset at herself for the morbid turn of her thoughts. She had encountered some horrible murders the last few years, the Last Supper reenactment instantly sprang to mind. However, none of those experiences had prepared her to see carnival masks made out of real human skin.

"Where were Mark and Geanie?" Jeremiah asked suddenly, interrupting her thoughts.

"They weren't in the hotel?" she asked.

He shook his head slowly. "I saw Joseph and Traci, but not the other two."

Cindy pulled out her phone. "I'll text the group and see what's going on," she said.

It was odd that Mark and Geanie were the ones missing. It would have made more sense if it was Mark and Traci since they were married. Of the four, Mark and Geanie, though, were best equipped to handle themselves in a fight.

Geanie had made that quite clear during all their practicing with Jeremiah.

Is everyone okay? Where are Mark and Geanie? she texted.

A moment later she added, Jeremiah and I are on a trolley following the guy from the hotel room.

She waited, staring at her phone, expecting a response. As the seconds rolled by she felt a growing uneasiness which turned to full-blown anxiety when five minutes passed and no one had responded. Mark never went anywhere without his phone and he was always very quick to respond. So was Geanie.

She glanced anxiously at Jeremiah. "Do you think something's happened to them?" she whispered.

~

Mark didn't like any part of this. Gerald's kidnappers were running them in circles and they were getting garbled texts from Joseph. Something wasn't right here.

"Ram the van," Geanie said.

"Excuse me?" Mark and the taxi driver asked simultaneously.

"I'll give you fifty thousand dollars to stop that van," Geanie said, her words clipped and cold.

"Yes, ma'am!" the driver said gleefully.

"What are you doing?" Mark demanded as the driver sped up.

"You can throw money or time at a problem and we're out of time," Geanie said, her voice somewhat detached.

"You're crazy!"

"Hold on!" the cabbie shouted as he yanked hard on the steering wheel.

The car started to spin and moments later there was a loud bang and the car stopped, throwing Mark forward. This time he did smack his head on the divider, and he struggled for a moment to remain conscious.

He heard a car door open followed by the sound of a woman shouting. He looked over and saw that Geanie had left the cab. He struggled to follow, noticing as he did so that the driver's airbag had deployed, knocking the man out.

Should have rammed from the side, Mark thought as he staggered toward the van. This whole thing was a mistake. He didn't even have a weapon on him.

He cleared the back of the cab just in time to see Geanie yank open the van door. Fear filled him as he half-expected a shot to ring out. Instead Geanie stumbled back a couple of feet and then looked wildly around. The driver staggered out of the van and started to come around toward them.

"Don't you move!" Mark roared, pointing at the man and wishing he was doing so with a gun and not just his finger.

"Where is he?" Geanie suddenly screamed, so loud it made Mark's ears hurt.

"What are you talking about, lady?" the van's driver asked.

"Gerald! Where is he?"

Mark came up beside Geanie and saw that the van was empty. He swore as he slammed his hand into the side of the vehicle in frustration.

"We've been had," he said. "Either they found a way to offload him under our noses or Gerald was never in here."

“Who are you talking about? And look what you did to my van!” the driver said, incensed.

Mark’s thoughts felt like they were going into overdrive.

“Who paid you?” he demanded.

“What?” the driver asked.

“Who paid you to drive around and lead us on a wild goose chase?”

“I don’t know what you’re-”

Geanie shoved the guy against the passenger side door.

“You are in a lot of trouble,” she hissed.

“What are you talking about?” the guy asked, his bravado weakening for a second.

“Conspiracy to commit kidnapping for starters. You better pray that doesn’t get upped to conspiracy to commit murder,” Mark said in the voice he reserved for the toughest criminals he had to interrogate.

“Kidnapping? Murder? Hey, I don’t know anything about-”

“Who paid you?”

The man swallowed hard and then finally sagged in defeat. “Some crazy chick. She said it was part of a game, like a road rally kind of thing. She offered me a thousand dollars to drive around and not lose you.”

“Did she already pay you?” Geanie demanded.

“Half. She told me I could pick up the other half from her about an hour from now.”

“Where?”

“At this house in the Garden District. That’s where she said the rally was ending.”

He rattled off an address and Mark looked at Geanie. That was where they were expected to be in an hour for whatever surprise Matthews had in store for them. Knowing that, hopefully they could ruin his plans, maybe show up early, capture him, and finally put an end to all this. Of course, they still didn't know what had happened to Gerald, where he was and who had him. He could feel sweat beading on his forehead as he got a sick feeling in his gut that no matter what move they made next someone was going to pay the price.

"Can I go?" the van driver whined.

Mark stared at him intently. It was possible he was telling the truth, that he was a random stranger that had been enlisted to give them the runaround. Then again, he might well be a confederate of Matthews and his people. He glanced at Geanie. She was clearly thinking the same thing but was waiting for him to make the decision.

Suddenly, he heard a siren and saw flashing lights. A police car was driving up. He gritted his teeth in anger, wishing he hadn't delayed. Now none of them were free to go anywhere.

16

Mark was aware that his phone had been buzzing in his pocket for a couple of minutes. He didn't dare reach for it with uniformed police climbing out of their car. They might think he was reaching for a weapon with tragic results.

"I am Detective Mark Walters of Pine Springs PD," he said in a calm, clear voice. "I've been working locally with Detectives Lewis and Moretti."

"Well, we'll find out in about half a minute if you're lying. They're almost on scene," the lead officer, a slender, balding man with a perpetual squint said, his tone wary.

"I'm happy to wait," Mark said.

In truth he was chafing at the delay, but it would do him no good to reveal that. Not now.

Geanie looked like she was on the verge of losing it. He sympathized, but he couldn't have her go off half-cocked.

"It's going to be okay," he said softly to her.

Every inch of her body seemed to be vibrating with barely suppressed adrenaline. He could see rage and frustration written all over her face and he just hoped she didn't do something that would get them both arrested.

Or killed.

"We'll get this all figured out," he continued.

"I hate this city," she muttered. "I wish we'd never come here."

"You're not alone in that."

The two police officers just continued to stare at them suspiciously. It was intolerable given the fact that every second wasted was another second head start Matthew and his lackeys had on them.

They had never actually seen Gerald when they got to the hospital. The information Joseph had gotten and passed on to them was that Gerald had been taken away in the van that his and Geanie's taxi driver had just successfully run off the road.

So, either there was a huge mix-up, or someone had lied to Joseph.

Or Joseph lied to us.

He felt like a traitor the moment the thought entered his brain. Joseph had never given him any reason to doubt him.

He has an account in that bank that Not Paul used…the one where the bankers are willing to kill to protect their clients' secrets.

Mark still had the knife scar to prove it. He'd found it more than a little disturbing to discover that Joseph had something he was willing to protect that way. Still, knowing Joseph's net worth it was probably something that belonged in a museum, something like a Hope diamond. At any rate it was ridiculous to speculate on. Whatever Joseph had in that bank, Mark was sure it was completely legal and respectable. Just like Joseph.

Who I saw hack into credit card records after using a worm he got off the dark web.

A shiver went up Mark's spine. Even Geanie had been surprised that her husband knew how to do those things. What else was the billionaire hiding from his wife and the rest of them?

What if he was one of the kidnapped children?

Mark's stomach twisted into knots. Joseph's family was the richest in the area and had deep roots in the community. If the cult Matthews had been running years before had been kidnapping the children of wealthy families in the area, how could they have passed up Joseph? To make it more tempting, Joseph's family were devout churchgoers, just like the Dryer family. Given Matthews' seeming grudge against religiously minded people like his pastor father-in-law, it would make sense he would have targeted Joseph. He would have been the right age and everything.

But there would have been some mention of Joseph Coulter in all the reports from that time. Unless…

With the Coulters' money and connections, they could have covered the whole thing up to avoid scandal and curiosity seekers.

"No," Mark whispered to himself.

"What?" Geanie asked.

"Sorry, nothing, just thinking," he said hastily.

None of the other children who had been kidnapped had been returned. The only family who got their child back was the Dryers and they didn't get their son, Paul. They got a changeling, Matthews' son, instead.

What if Matthews had more than one son?

Mark felt like everything around him was spinning. He slowly lowered himself down to a sitting position on the curb as sweat began pouring off him.

"Mark, are you alright?" he heard Geanie ask. Her voice sounded miles away.

He wanted to answer, to tell her he was fine or that he just needed a moment to catch his breath. He wanted to tell her anything except what was running through his head.

Joseph's parents had both died when he was a teenager. Mark tried to remember if he'd ever heard how. He thought maybe it was some kind of an accident.

What if it wasn't?

What if the reason Matthews seemed to know their every move was because one of his own children was in their very midst? Mark struggled to think about the couple of times that he'd seen Paul and Joseph in the same room together. Had there ever been any sense of familiarity or shared looks between them? If so, had Paul been bitter that he had been slotted into a far less wealthy family than Joseph with no control of the money himself?

Geanie sat down next to him and put her hand on his shoulder, making Mark jump.

"Where are you right now?" she whispered.

"I'm down the rabbit hole," he admitted.

"That's not a safe place to go," she said.

He looked up and into her eyes. In that moment he saw the same doubts and fears he was having mirrored there.

"Not a safe place at all," she said, her face strained, skin unnaturally pale.

"How long have you suspected?" he breathed.

"Not long."

There was so much they needed to say, so much they needed to talk about. At that moment, though, the detectives they had been waiting for finally arrived. All Mark could think was that they'd taken more than thirty seconds to arrive like the patrolman had told them and that Lewis and her partner had picked the worst possible moment to show up.

He stared at Geanie.

"I know," she said. "It's…"

"Yes, it is."

He stood up slowly, not trusting his legs to support his weight. He struggled to put on his game face. He couldn't let the other detectives know there was something wrong. He glanced over at the van with the taxi wedged into its side.

Well, nothing wrong other than the obvious.

"Detective Walters, why am I not surprised to see you here?" Detective Lewis asked with a smile that did not reach her lovely eyes.

"Because this is New Orleans, and, like half the residents, you're probably psychic," he said as casually as he could.

"Nice try," she said, smiling a little more.

Her partner was busy inspecting the van and the taxi. Mark could see him walking around, viewing things from every angle.

"How about we cut to the chase, and you let me in on the secret of what happened at this particular location?"

"I'd be happy to," Mark said, forcing his own smile.

"In that case enlighten me, or, at least, entertain me."

Mark quickly filled her in. It was not ideal given that she was questioning him and Geanie at the same time. He occasionally winced at some of her answers, wishing she had phrased them differently. She wasn't a cop, though, and so he couldn't expect her to think like one. Mark did manage to stress that their cab driver should not be held accountable for what he did because he was doing as instructed to try and save a man's life.

"Even if that man turned out not to be in the van he rammed into," Lorraine noted dryly.

"Exactly. He had no way to know that, just as we had no way to know," Mark said.

"How much did you offer to pay him?" Moretti asked, coming up behind Mark and causing him to jump ever so slightly.

"Nothing," Mark said.

"Whatever it took," Geanie said at the same time.

Mark winced. Another inconvenient answer they were going to have to deal with, particularly if the other detectives decided to play hardball with them.

"Basically, you're telling me that your little war with this man Matthews has now spilled onto the streets of my city," Lorraine said.

He wanted to contradict her as there was so much that was wrong with what she'd just said. However, that wouldn't help them at the moment.

"Yes," he said.

"I see. And I'm supposed to tolerate this because…?"

"Because you hate to see a real criminal flout the system as he has and get away with it for decades."

"You are correct," she said.

"So, help me catch this guy and then we'll both be out of your hair," Mark said with his most winning smile.

"Well, at least the case of the rundown van is officially solved," Lorraine said with a sigh as she glanced at the van while putting her notepad away.

"No. We still don't have an answer to the most important question," Geanie said bluntly. "Where is Gerald Wilson?"

~

Cindy was looking worried. Not being able to get hold of Mark and Geanie clearly had her spooked. Jeremiah wasn't far behind her. Normally he wouldn't have worried too much. Mark could handle himself in most situations and Geanie had been his best student for survival fighting. Nothing about the last few days had been normal, though.

He thought of calling Joseph to at least find out where Mark and Geanie had gone, but he knew he had to focus. They were on the same trolley as their quarry, and he couldn't afford to allow himself to split focus even for a second. Doing so could prove fatal. They were fortunate in that people got on at every stop. Otherwise, with all the people getting off, it would have become impossible to hide from the man they were following.

"Man" didn't seem to be quite the appropriate word to describe the hulking figure that had attacked him. His opponent was old enough physically, but clearly still had the mind of a child trapped inside him through some kind of psychological trauma. It made it difficult to think of him as an adult and not a lost, helpless kid.

He winced as he felt the bruising along his jawline, a grim reminder that the other might be lost, but he was not necessarily helpless.

Danny Monroe.

The name sprung into his mind. He'd been wracking his brain for the last half hour trying to remember what Mark had said about the kids that were still missing from the Green Pastures cult site. The detective had said that Danny Monroe's body hadn't been recovered. There were a couple of others still unaccounted for besides Danny and Sadie, but those were the names Mark had actually said out loud. When they came face-to-face again, as would be inevitable,

Jeremiah would call the man-child by the name Danny and see how he responded.

"Do you think we're heading to the Garden District?" Cindy asked softly.

Jeremiah nodded. It seemed the most logical destination at this point. If Danny was indeed acting on Jeremiah's suggestion that he go home, then this could mean that Matthews had a home in the Garden District. The prestige and opulence of the area would no doubt please the type of personality that would set himself up as a cult leader. Still, it was a far more visible place than Jeremiah would have anticipated. As much as Matthews might crave the spotlight, the man also had plenty of reason and need to keep out of it, lest he be discovered and put into prison at long last.

Of course, it was possible the District was just the place where Danny would get off and start on a long walk to a different location. Jeremiah didn't think so, though. Indeed, he felt that they were closing in on their quarry.

He glanced at Cindy. The look of animation on her face told him that she was also anticipating that things were about to explode into motion.

Steady. Don't jump the gun, he cautioned himself. It wouldn't do him any good to make assumptions at this point, particularly since Mathews had already managed to defy so many assumptions about him.

"Are you okay?" Cindy asked.

"Yes. Just thinking, planning," he whispered back. He wished he wasn't putting her in harm's way by bringing her with him, but in this city he hadn't yet figured out where he could put her that would be out of harm's way.

Not that she'd stay there even if he did find that place. She was stubborn that way.

"Do you think he's really going home?"

"I do," Jeremiah said, letting himself sound more confident than he felt.

"And do you think Matthews will be there?" she asked.

Jeremiah took a deep breath. That was a tough question. On the one hand, he hoped so because that would give him a chance to finish this. On the other hand, he was worried that if the man was there then this was a trap for them.

He thought about turning on the feature on his phone to allow it to be tracked easily. Joseph would clearly know how to if the need arose. He ultimately chose not to. He'd gone through the effort of dismantling a lot of things on their phones so they couldn't be hacked or tracked and it was best to leave them that way. Still, he wished he didn't have the growing sense of walking into a trap without backup. No one knew where they were or what they were doing. Hopefully that didn't become a fatal problem.

He looked at Cindy. She was waiting for an answer about whether or not he thought that they were heading for Matthews' home.

"I don't know," he admitted. "We're just going to have to take this one step at time."

As it turned out, a couple of stops later Danny did indeed get off in the Garden District. Jeremiah and Cindy followed carefully behind, but he never once looked behind him. That was good for them, but it worried Jeremiah a bit. The way Danny kept striding single-mindedly forward was almost deliberate. He didn't turn and look at things and people he was passing by even reflexively. It was like he was determined not to look around.

Jeremiah started to slow. A mosquito bit the back of his neck, but he scarcely felt it. He was too busy thinking about Danny's behavior. It was unnatural. Then again, the man-child wasn't exactly normal, so maybe he was expecting him to react too much like other people. What he should be doing…

He blinked and the world went a bit fuzzy. He stopped.

"Something's not-" Jeremiah started to say. His tongue felt thick and his limbs were going numb. He looked at Cindy and could see a slow paralysis creeping across her face.

He was in the middle of crying out to God for help when he could feel himself falling. Darkness descended and he felt hands grabbing at him but there was nothing he could do about it.

~

Cindy's vision was blurring but she could still see the three masked figures who grabbed Jeremiah and threw him into the back of a black van. She expected them to come back for her, but they climbed in after Jeremiah. She tried to turn her head, fighting to stay conscious. Surely there was someone else who was there to pick her up and carry her to the van. They had to mean to kidnap both of them, not just one of them. She was struggling to keep awake. Suddenly, the vehicle took off with a scream of tires. She lay on the sidewalk, tears leaking from her eyes.

17

Mark stared intently at Geanie. She'd asked a good question. They'd been chasing the van around thinking they were rescuing Gerald. Since he wasn't in the van, where was he?

Detective Lewis pulled out her phone and called the hospital. After a brief conversation with an administrator and a slightly longer one with what sounded like a nurse, she ended the call and turned back to them.

"It's confirmed that he was supposed to be discharged to a facility set up to help with rehabilitation. Supposedly a representative from there picked him up."

"You might want to check that," Mark said tensely.

Lorraine checked her phone and then made another call. Her face turned grim, and she finally ended that call.

"The driver and nurse they sent out got a flat tire. It's still being repaired. They haven't made it to the hospital."

"That flat was no accident," Mark said.

"That's what I was thinking," Lorraine said.

"So, who picked him up and where did they take him?" Geanie asked.

"Good question. I'm going to head to the hospital and see if I can find some answers," Lorraine said.

"If you don't mind, we'd like to go with you," Mark told her.

She narrowed her eyes. "Trouble seems to follow you."

"More like I find it. Trouble is already happening. Don't you want someone with you who has a better than even chance of dealing with it?" he asked.

"Fine, but remember, you're a civilian in my town."

"Yes, ma'am," Mark replied.

Three minutes later he and Geanie were in the backseat of Lorraine and her partner's car. He didn't like sitting in the back of a police vehicle, even if it was a detective's car, but there wasn't any help for it. At least they were on their way to the hospital and, hopefully, answers.

~

Cindy's vision was still swimming before her eyes as she heard running footsteps. People were surrounding her. She could hear excited voices, including one of them shouting.

"Call 911!"

She struggled to stay conscious, to force her fingers to the cell phone in her pocket, but she just couldn't. As everything faded to black the sound of sirens was the last thing she heard.

~

In the back of the police vehicle, Mark finally had a moment to check his phone. His blood turned cold as he saw the messages from Joseph.

"What's wrong?" Geanie whispered, having not checked her phone yet.

Mark shook his head sharply and called Joseph. He didn't like the fact that Lorraine and her partner would be able to overhear the conversation, but it couldn't wait.

"Where are you?" Joseph demanded.

"On the way to the hospital. Again."

"What! Why?"

"To look for Gerald. He wasn't in the van we thought he was. What's going on there?"

"Trouble. One of Matthews' children attacked us. Jeremiah interrupted and then both of them took off. I haven't heard from him or Cindy since then. I've been trying to reach her and you and Geanie."

"Geanie's here with me. We've got Detectives Lewis and Moretti here with us," Mark said by way of warning.

"Great," Joseph said sarcastically. "Because they've been a huge help."

"There's still time," Mark muttered. "Is Traci okay?" he asked more loudly.

"She's fine, just shaken up. That monster didn't have a chance to touch her."

"Are you okay?"

"I'll live," Joseph said, anger in his voice. "So much for my weeks of training. It did no good."

Mark winced. Apparently when confronted with actual danger Joseph hadn't managed to do as Jeremiah had taught them. That was unfortunate, but not entirely unexpected. Honestly, of all of them he had the most faith that Geanie would be able to perform under stress. After seeing how she'd handled the last hour, he was even more certain of it.

Mark could see the hospital through the side window as they turned into it.

"Joseph, I have to go. I'll call you back when I know something."

The main entrance to the hospital was within visual range of the emergency room. Detective Moretti pulled up at the same time an ambulance did. Mark climbed out of the car and was about to head inside when the hairs on the back of his neck stood on end.

Joseph had said he couldn't get hold of either Jeremiah or Cindy. If Jeremiah was chasing after the man, then that made sense. But what about Cindy?

He turned and started walking toward the ambulance, his heart filling with dread. He hoped he was wrong, but with every step he took he became more certain. He was nearly at the ambulance when they opened the back doors and unloaded a woman on a gurney whose face was pale and still as death.

It was Cindy.

~

"The rules are very simple and very clear," Matthews said as he bent over Jeremiah who was securely tied to an uncomfortable metal chair.

Jeremiah stared intently at the other man, struggling to clear his head of the remaining fog from the tranquilizers. Matthews didn't look like a psychopathic killer. In fact, he looked very much like an older version of Not Paul. The big difference was a handful of wrinkles and the eyes. The eyes held a kind of light in them that wasn't quite natural. Jeremiah had seen that light before in the eyes of fanatics, many of whom he had killed for his country.

"My children have your lovely fiancée at a separate location. If you try to escape, they kill her. If you try to hurt me, they kill her. Do you understand?"

"Yes," Jeremiah said, holding in the anger that he was feeling. That anger wouldn't do him or Cindy any good in the present situation.

"And just so I'm perfectly clear, they won't kill her quickly. My children…enjoy…their work. Almost too much," Matthews said with a twisted smile.

Matthews and his children, they were all mad dogs who needed to be put down before they could harm anyone else or make any new converts. Jeremiah vowed to himself that he would see to it personally.

Matthews eventually left the room, flipping off the lights as he did. It didn't matter. Jeremiah had already memorized the layout of the room. The twelve-by-twelve room had bare concrete walls. A large window on one of them had been covered. The floor had shown some discoloration where a desk and some filing cabinets had likely stood for a long time. Everything he saw, indeed the very smell of the air in the room, led him to believe that he was in an office inside a warehouse.

That meant if he escaped this room there would likely be multiple exits to take once he was on the warehouse floor. Most or all would be locked, guarded, or alarmed even. That wouldn't matter much. He was good at making short work of locks, guards, and alarms. None could stand in his way for any length of time.

The only thing keeping him in that warehouse, in the office, in the very chair he was restrained in was him. He knew that and seemingly so did Matthews. That was why he was holding Cindy at some other location. The threat to her was far more effective than any restraints or any closed doors could ever be.

Of course, Matthews could be lying. He might have Cindy in the same warehouse he was in. Given that was a possibility, Jeremiah couldn't risk leaving the warehouse without first searching for her. That would take time and would greatly improve the chances of him being discovered and, therefore, the chance that Matthews or one of his followers could get to her and hurt her.

Then again, maybe Matthews didn't have her in this warehouse or anywhere. He might have just kidnapped him. Jeremiah shook his head. He knew that Cindy had also been hit with the tranquilizer darts. He'd seen her fall before he'd been grabbed. It would have been downright wasteful of Matthews to leave such a valuable hostage behind.

Unless he just killed her outright.

Dark thoughts swirled through Jeremiah's mind, torturing him with images from his deepest nightmares. He tried to push them back down. After all, he was the hostage here. It wasn't him that Matthews was obsessed with. Mark had been Not Paul's partner. He and Matthews' son had been close. He was the one who had discovered the existence and identity of Matthews' grandson. It made sense that Matthews was obsessed with him.

But why was he obsessed with Cindy? She had received the first mask when they arrived in New Orleans. Cindy had only had a handful of interactions with Paul over the course of a year and three murder investigations. There hadn't been anything especially meaningful about those. Why target her? After all, Jeremiah himself had arguably had a deeper connection to Not Paul. He'd been the one that was there when Paul was killed.

Jeremiah suddenly wondered why Matthews hadn't asked him about it. Presumably Matthews knew how Paul died. After all, he seemed to know an awful lot that went on in and around Pine Springs as it related to his son. Knowing something from reading a report or hearing about it was never as fulfilling as hearing about it firsthand from someone who witnessed it.

That's why the apostles wrote the Gospels, to tell their story firsthand to those whom they couldn't reach to speak it to.

The thought ambushed him, startling him. He had no idea why he should be thinking about that now. He tried to shove it back down into his subconscious, realizing he was going to have to do some serious self-questioning later.

The point was, Matthews should want to hear from Jeremiah himself what happened to Paul. Maybe that was why Matthews had kidnapped him and not one of the others.

Jeremiah thought back to the hotel room. Matthews' "son", the man Jeremiah was assuming was Danny, had attacked Joseph and Traci. To what purpose? Was it to kill them or had he had the intent of kidnapping one or both of them?

Jeremiah shook his head. The man hadn't had a tranquilizer gun on him. He was sure of that. For that matter, Danny hadn't had any weapon on him. If he had, he would have used it in the fight. And he didn't have any obvious means of getting an unconscious body downstairs unobserved. There hadn't been a laundry cart or food trolley or even a giant duffel bag with which he could disguise a whole person, let alone two.

It was possible he'd been told to go and escape and lead people on a chase after him. He'd been so casual about it, though, that Jeremiah had a hard time believing that was the case. It would have required a level of subterfuge ability that Jeremiah doubted the damaged personality he had encountered was capable of.

Jeremiah forced himself to take a mental step back even farther. His and Cindy's decision to go visit Jordan wasn't something that Matthews could have easily anticipated. It was possible that Danny had arrived at that hotel room expecting to see Jeremiah and Cindy there as well as Joseph and Traci. Any of the four of them, or all of them, could have been his intended target. But then why send him in unarmed? Was Matthews that confident of his adopted son's abilities or that underestimating of theirs?

And what of Mark and Geanie? Where were they? Jeremiah still didn't know the answer to that. Had Matthews already managed to draw the two of them off on a wild goose chase before Danny got to the hotel?

There were too many unknown factors, and it was starting to really frustrate Jeremiah. He didn't like it when he didn't understand the enemy's plans and movements. No one did, but he always took special offense. He should be able to see the big picture, figure out what Matthews was planning.

Matthews is a mad man.

Maybe that was the key, the difference that made all the difference. Matthews didn't think like an ordinary man. Therefore, in order to outsmart him, neither could Jeremiah.

Jeremiah took a deep breath and felt a tremor in his soul.

There was a place inside him, a deep, dark place that he'd only gone once before that was as close to madness as he ever wanted to be. It frightened him, that corner of him. It frightened him so much that he never talked about it, never even let himself think about it.

When he'd first joined the military, he'd seen a five-year-old girl killed by a terrorist. It was a brutal, random act that had shocked him to his very core. Growing up in Israel there were days when the rockets fired at the country numbered in the hundreds, and he had thought he was used to death and uncertainty or savagery. He hadn't been.

Not until he'd seen the little girl torn apart so casually.

It had sparked something in him, a rage that had first burned hot then so cold that it filled him with a kind of emptiness, a dark hollowness. He had acted. He had....

He turned his thoughts away from it as he always did whenever they strayed too close to that horrible time.

What had come out of it had changed his life forever. That's when the Mossad had approached him, given him a purpose, a target for that anger that he felt. They set him loose and let him do what he did best until the anger slowly faded, replaced by determination and even more coldness. A coldness that had not thawed until he met Cindy.

Cindy had brought light and warmth back to his world. That and a thousand other reasons was why he went nearly berserk when anything or anyone dared threaten her in the least. In his heart he felt her innocence, her purity. It was like she was that five-year-old girl restored and transfigured into an angel of salvation and light. She was his to hold and protect and if he could do so then the darkness could never come for him again. That she could possibly love him despite everything had been an unexpected blessing, so great that the enormity of it nearly crushed him at times and terrified him at others. He couldn't slip into madness. Not while she lived. He could never let her see that.

He realized after a few moments that tears had been running freely down his cheeks, for how long he did not know. He took a shuddering breath, tasting the salt on his lips. There were times when a man had to face his own soul and he always fiercely avoided facing his.

They had been in worse places than this. They had faced more imminent death. Why then should he be so moved by his current circumstances?

Because he was afraid.

He was afraid not just of losing Cindy and the others. He was afraid of losing himself.

Again.

That knowledge shone through the darkness like a beacon of light.

Do not be afraid.

The words came to him, whispered in his mind in a voice that was not his own. There was something familiar about the voice, and he knew he'd heard it at least once before. Something touched his left shoulder, but instead of jerking away, he felt himself leaning into the touch. It felt like Cindy's touch, but it was not. There were similarities, but this was stronger and somehow even warmer. Sitting there in the darkness he could feel compassion and warmth around him.

My child.

The tears began to come even harder.

Let not your heart be troubled: ye believe in God, believe also in me.

He recognized the words. They were from the Christian Bible. From one of the Gospels that had come to mind earlier.

He began to shake from head to toe with an emotion he did not recognize. Fear, excitement, awe. It was all of those and none of those and yet it transcended them. He sobbed openly.

"Who are you?" he cried out.

I Am who I Am.

"Why? Why are you revealing yourself to me?" he asked.

You imagine yourself alone and you are finally quiet enough to listen.

"Tell me what I should do."

Love me and feed my sheep.

Then the presence was gone, and it made him want to weep even harder for the loss. Something in his mind told him, though, that the presence he had sensed, that had spoken to him, was not gone but was all around him, supporting him, watching him, loving him.

"Just because you can't see G-d doesn't mean He's not there," he whispered to himself.

But why had G-d spoken to him with those words? Why had He chosen that way in which to reveal Himself?

"G-d does nothing by accident," he told himself. "There is nothing random in His acts."

And clarity flooded his mind. He understood. Perhaps it was G-d, perhaps it was the memory of his own terrible experience, but he knew why Matthews had sent Danny to that hotel room. It didn't have anything to do with which people were and were not there. It wasn't about kidnapping or killing anyone. It was seemingly random violence aimed at specific targets to cause one effect.

The spread of terror and confusion.

18

Jeremiah's revelation, while causing great personal relief, still didn't answer the original question he'd had, though. Why had Matthews not asked him about his son. Was he waiting? He didn't seem like the type who would delay gratification like that. His curiosity must be killing him. Was it possible he didn't know that Jeremiah had been there when Not Paul was killed?

Jeremiah resolved to figure out why the other man hadn't asked and to see what he could do to use the information against him. For now, though, all he could do was wait.

"I hate waiting," he whispered to the darkness.

~

Geanie came running up to Mark.

"Who is it?" she called before she was close enough to see the stretcher.

"Cindy!" he called out.

"You know this woman?" one of the EMTs asked.

"Very well," Mark said.

"Great, come inside with us."

"I'll go," Geanie quickly spoke up. "Mark, you should go see if you can find out what happened to Gerald."

He reluctantly agreed even though in that moment he was a lot more interested in finding out what had happened to Cindy.

And Jeremiah. Where is he? Why isn't he here?

Mark was trying not to let his imagination get the better of him.

"Was there a man with her?" he asked the EMT.

"No. She was by herself it looks like. She had collapsed on the sidewalk and a bystander called 911. It looks like someone hit her with a tranquilizer."

The EMTs hurried Cindy inside and Geanie ran beside them. Once they were gone Mark forced himself to head back to the waiting detectives.

"Who was it?" Moretti asked.

"Cindy. Someone shot her with a tranquilizer," Mark said.

"Rough," Moretti commented.

"Why?" Lorraine asked, looking surprised.

"To get her out of the way, maybe."

"Out of the way of what?" Lorraine asked.

"Of them taking Jeremiah," Mark said grimly.

"What do you mean? How can you know that?" Moretti asked quickly, suspicion lacing his voice.

"Simple. He's not with her. That leaves two options. He's dead or they took him prisoner when they shot her. Since his body wasn't discovered near her, I'm guessing it's the latter."

He was also hoping and praying it was the latter.

"What reason would Matthews have to take him prisoner?" Lorraine asked with a scowl.

"Why do psychopaths do anything?" Mark asked. He took a deep breath. "I'm guessing it's all part of his sick, twisted plan."

~

Half an hour later Mark was still working with the detectives and the hospital staff to try and figure out what might have happened to Gerald. Geanie called and he answered quickly.

"How's Cindy?" he asked.

"Awake. They have her in a secure room at the far end of one of the wings. There's only one way in and out of the area."

"Good, maybe we can hold onto her that way," Mark growled.

"How is it going with you?"

"Lousy. We're still no closer to figuring out where they took Wilson. All we know is that a big, burly guy in a uniform showed up to get him. The only decent description I'm getting of him is that he was in a hurry."

"Not much to go on," Geanie said sympathetically.

"No."

"I called Joseph. He's still pretty shaken up, but he promises me that he and Traci are doing okay."

Mark barely stifled a curse.

"What's wrong?" Geanie asked sharply.

"Traci. I should have called to check on her."

"It's fine. She's fine."

"Yeah, but I should have heard that with my own ears."

"She knows you're up to your ears in the search," Geanie said softly.

"Doesn't make me less of a lousy husband. My wife gets attacked and I forget to call and ask how she's doing."

"Take it easy, Mark."

"Right. This from the lady who was flinging thousands of dollars at a cab driver not that long ago."

He could hear Geanie sigh over the phone. "We all have our stress points," she said.

"That's true," he said, a thought occurring to him. "Let me call you back."

He hung up and walked back to talk to the nurse who'd had dealings with the man who picked up Wilson. She looked up and frowned when she saw him coming.

"I'm sorry. I haven't been able to think of anything I haven't already told you. I wish I could be more help," she said.

"It's fine. I just wanted to go back over a couple of things. You said he seemed like he was in a rush?"

She nodded. "He kept looking at his watch and muttering that he couldn't be late. He seemed quite agitated about it when it took us a few minutes to get a wheelchair to transport Mr. Wilson."

"Did you recover that wheelchair outside or anywhere else?" Mark asked.

"I don't know, exactly. It's not like I logged a number or anything. We usually don't pay attention to that sort of thing."

"And you say he wore a watch?"

"Yes. It was one of those digital watches. I haven't seen one in ages. Most people I know just use their phones anymore."

"You said he was a big guy?"

"Yes. Very strong, but not like he worked out. I'll be honest, I didn't pay as much attention to him as I should have. I'm actually studying to be a psychologist and I was busy trying to diagnose him."

"Diagnose him?" Mark asked sharply.

"Yes. He didn't seem quite…right."

"What, like he was crazy or something?"

"More like slow, not completely there."

Mark thought about Sadie and how she had seemingly reverted to moments when she was childlike. This might be another one of Matthews' "children". There were a couple of kids still unaccounted for, including Danny Monroe.

"Thank you," he said. "Good luck with school."

"Thanks," she said with a bright smile.

Mark moved off a safe distance and called Joseph.

"Everything okay?" Joseph asked tensely.

"Working on it. Can you tell me what the guy who attacked you looked like?"

"He was a big guy, strong like an ox and fast, but you wouldn't have thought so to look at him."

"Heavyset?" Mark asked.

"A little."

"And did he seem slow or off?"

"Yes. How did you know?"

"I'm thinking the guy who attacked you is the same guy who grabbed Gerald Wilson."

There was a pause on the other end of the line. Finally, Joseph spoke up. "The hotel's not that far from the hospital. I suppose, technically, if he came straight here from the hospital, he could have made it in time. But I don't think he would have had any time to stop anywhere."

"That's what I wanted to hear."

Mark started to hang up then winced. "Sorry, can you put Traci on the phone?"

"She's in the bathroom throwing up. I think she's pretty stressed out."

"Well, tell her I called to see how she's doing," Mark said.

"I will."

Mark headed back to the nurse's station.

"Back so soon?" the nurse said with a smile.

"Yeah, just one more thing."

"You sound like that old TV detective. Columbus?"

"Columbo," Mark corrected her. "Thanks."

"So, what is it?"

"Once you got the wheelchair and got Wilson in it, did you accompany him and the guy from the care facility outside?"

"No. He took charge of the wheelchair and then Mrs. Beltran started shouting in her room. I ran in to check on her and found that she was having a nightmare. I got her settled back down and when I came out of her room, Wilson and the man were gone."

"Which way were they headed when you last saw them?"

"Toward the elevators. From there they would have gone down to the first floor. There's a long hallway, then a turn to the right, another to the left, and you're in the main lobby."

"Thank you very much," he said.

"I wish I could have been of more help."

"Oh, you were great," he said as he headed toward the elevators.

Danny, or whoever the man had been, would have at least headed down to the first floor. Mark rode the elevator down and then stepped off. There were restrooms to the left and then a long hallway that stretched down to the right. He stepped toward the hallway then turned. He stared at the restrooms for a moment. There was one for men, one for women, and then a family restroom. The family restroom had a little red occupied sign on the lock. He tried it and discovered that the handle was indeed locked.

He knocked loudly. "Hello?"

He listened, but there was no answer.

He pounded his fist on the door. "Hello!" he shouted.

Again, there was only silence.

The elevator doors opened, and an orderly stepped out.

"You!" Mark said, loudly enough that he startled the poor man.

"What?"

"I need someone who can get this door open. I think there's someone trapped inside," Mark said.

The orderly frowned and pushed past him. He tried the door and, finding it locked, pounded loudly. "Are you alright in there?"

When there was no answer, he turned to Mark with a frown. "Are you sure someone's in there?"

Mark was by no means sure, but he wasn't going to admit that. "The door's locked from the inside, isn't it?"

The orderly nodded and grabbed a walkie talkie off his belt. "I'll get someone down here right away."

~

Matthews came back a while later and tied Jeremiah more securely to the chair. It didn't matter. Jeremiah could still escape whenever he wanted, whenever he felt it was safe for Cindy that he did. When Matthews turned to go Jeremiah spoke up.

"Why haven't you asked me about your son?"

Matthews stopped, his hand on the door.

"Don't you want to know?" Jeremiah pressed.

"Know what?" Matthews asked without turning around.

"Everything. How he lived. Who he was. What he thought about. …How he died."

"I know how he died," Matthews said, still not turning.

Jeremiah could hear the change in the man's breathing. It had accelerated slightly.

"You might know what killed him and where, but that really doesn't tell you much, does it?" Jeremiah said.

"He died at Green Pastures. Ironic. Poetic even," the man said in a slightly sing-song voice. "All Pauls die there, the real and the fake." Matthews twisted the doorknob.

"Don't you want to know what was said, what was talked about before he died?" Jeremiah called.

Matthews froze. Several seconds passed and the only sound was that of Matthews' breathing which was growing even more shallow and rapid.

"You were there?" Matthews whispered at last.

A tigerish thrill raced through Jeremiah. He had gotten Matthews' attention and learned something very important. The man hadn't read the police report. He wasn't nearly as connected or omniscient as he seemed. Jeremiah smiled and leaned back in his chair. The balance of power had just shifted, and he was fully prepared to take advantage of it.

Jeremiah said nothing and at last Matthews turned toward him, his hand falling off the doorknob. He took half a dozen steps back toward Jeremiah and then stopped when they could see each other clearly. Matthews stared into his eyes, probing them. Jeremiah stared back, unflinching. A smile slowly spread across his face as he watched the other man searching, flailing, for the truth.

"You were there," Matthews finally said softly. It was a statement, not a question, as though he had seen the truth in Jeremiah's eyes.

"I was," Jeremiah confirmed.

"You saw what happened to him…my boy."

"I was with him. I held his body. I buried it to protect it from animals and the elements before it could be moved to its final location."

"That was a kindness."

"It was. He had done me one."

Matthews stood there, his breathing shallow and rapid. He clenched and unclenched his fists. He wanted to know, but he couldn't bring himself to ask. Asking would be a sign of weakness. Jeremiah felt the smile spread farther across his face as he observed the other man.

"Ask me," Jeremiah said.

Matthews licked his lips. He was not a man used to asking for anything, only commanding it.

"You will tell me," Matthews demanded, but there was a catch in his voice, accentuated by the shortness of breath he was experiencing.

"All you have to do is ask," Jeremiah said.

"Tell me. I demand that you do."

"Ask me."

"You will tell me what I need to know or I will hurt you," Matthews said, making himself try to appear taller.

"Amazing thing about me. The more I hurt, the less talkative I get," Jeremiah said. "Except, of course, to G-d. When I'm in pain I talk to Him loudly and frequently."

Matthews flinched. It was a small movement, but Jeremiah saw it. He had the man in a corner because Matthews desperately wanted to know about his son but didn't want to ask and didn't want to risk hearing Jeremiah call upon G-d in distress.

Everyone has their weakness.

Jeremiah had spent years studying people. Long enough to know that everyone was afraid of something and everyone wanted something. Knowing those two things could help you manipulate just about anyone so long as you knew what you were doing.

Jeremiah would give Matthews the information about Paul for a price. Cindy's freedom. Once he was sure she was safe it would be a simple matter to free himself and snap Matthews' neck. He continued to stare into Matthews' eyes, knowing that by refusing to blink he was starting to have a hypnotic effect on the other.

Matthews took a step forward. Then another.

Suddenly, the door slammed open, bouncing against the wall with a loud clang. Matthews jerked and spun toward the intruder even as Jeremiah cursed to himself.

Standing in the doorway was Sadie.

"Father, I've finished with the decorations. What do you want me to do next?" she asked.

Matthews walked toward her. "Come, I want to show you the mask I picked out to go with your party dress."

Matthews quickly escorted her out of the room, closing the door behind him, refusing to turn and look at Jeremiah. The moment had passed, and Jeremiah was unlikely to get another such opportunity. Matthews would be more guarded from now on. He might not even enter the room with Jeremiah by himself or even at all. He could easily send Sadie in if he needed something.

~

It took fifteen minutes, but someone finally showed up who could get the restroom unlocked. Mark had been pacing the entire time while he waited, praying that the delay wouldn't prove fatal.

"Did you see someone go in here?" the man asked.

"Not exactly," Mark said.

"Then how do you know-"

The man abruptly stopped talking as he swung the door open and saw what was inside. There, sitting in a wheelchair, was Gerald Wilson. His head had been bashed in.

19

Mark hit the wall in frustration with his fist and gave an angry shout. Then he sagged against the wall in defeat as the man who had opened the door began shouting into his walkie talkie. A minute later hospital staff were swarming down the hallway.

Mark was pushed back as Gerald's body was wheeled out of the bathroom. A doctor reached out and touched his throat.

"He's still alive! Move people!"

Mark felt hope surge through him even as more people jostled him. Gerald was quickly spirited away. He trailed behind until a nurse finally barred his way.

"He's under police protection. Don't let anyone see him without my permission," Mark said, quickly flashing his badge.

The nurse nodded understanding then disappeared inside the restricted area. Frustrated and more than a little worried Mark decided to head back upstairs.

He found Cindy in a private room at the end of a hall just like Geanie had said. Both Geanie and Detective Lewis were with her. Cindy was groggy looking, but at least she was sitting up.

"How are you feeling?" Mark asked.

"They took Jeremiah," she said. "Why would they take him and leave me behind?"

"I don't know," he admitted. He was relieved to hear that as far as she knew Jeremiah was still alive.

The detective was ending a phone call and the scowl she was wearing told him she had heard something that didn't please her.

"What is it?" he asked.

She hesitated.

"Look, we're going to need to work together to solve this," he said. "I know you're not used to working with civilians or out of town cops, but trust me, you can do worse as far as a taskforce goes."

Lorraine pursed her lips as though measuring his words. She slipped her phone into her jacket pocket and gave him a short nod.

"I just discovered something about the security guard who was murdered and had his face stolen."

"What?" Mark asked.

"He was going under an assumed name. In fact, his whole identity was fake."

"You mean he wasn't a security guard?" Geanie asked.

"No, he was, but his name, his driver's license, social security number, all of those were fake."

"So, he changed his name at some point. Hiding from something?" Mark guessed.

"Possibly. We haven't heard anything from Federal law enforcement, so as far as we know he wasn't in the witness relocation program. All we know at this point is that he wasn't who he pretended to be."

"Just like Paul," Cindy whispered.

A chill danced up Mark's spine.

"You think the security guard is the third mask, don't you?"

"It makes sense. We're still running DNA on it."

"So our three masks all belong to people who were not who they said they were?" Mark said.

"That is correct. So is what Matthews doing, a metaphor for unmasking them, their deception?" Lorraine asked.

"That sounds about right," Mark said, feeling himself begin to sweat.

"But why would he care if people were living under assumed identities?" Geanie asked. "After all, we know that he himself has done so more than once."

"Maybe he's tired of pretending to be someone he's not and wants to take his own masks off. Symbolically at least," Lorraine said.

Mark felt like he was going to be sick. The worst part was he couldn't talk about it in front of Lorraine. Ironic given his speech about them all working together, but there was a lot she couldn't know about them. He slowly turned his head to look at Cindy. From the look in her eyes, he realized she'd come to the same thought that he had. Matthews was skinning people who were living under assumed identities.

Jeremiah was living under an assumed identity.

He only hoped and prayed that somehow Matthews didn't know or hadn't guessed that. It might explain why he'd taken him but left Cindy behind.

"I don't feel good," Cindy whimpered.

"Probably a side effect of the tranquilizer in your system," Lorraine said. "It should work itself fully out within a day or two I would think." She then turned toward Mark. "Did you have any success tracking down Mr. Wilson?"

"Yes," Mark said. "The man who took him bashed him in the head and left him locked in a family restroom downstairs. Doctors are working on him now."

"That poor man!" Geanie blurted out. "Hasn't he been through enough already?"

"Apparently not as far as Matthews is concerned," Mark said grimly.

"That's not right," Geanie said, her face turning red as she clenched and unclenched her fists.

"How much longer do you have to stay?" Mark asked Cindy.

"They said they want to keep me a couple more hours."

"Hopefully by then we'll know something more about Gerald," Mark said.

"I hate waiting," Geanie said.

"Why don't you go back to the hotel and be with Joseph and Traci," he suggested.

He wasn't entirely sure it was safe, but since Matthews' lackey had already shown up there, hopefully, they'd steer clear for a while.

"I could drive you over," Lorraine offered.

"I would appreciate it," Geanie said.

"The city's taxi commission would also appreciate it," Lorraine said with the hint of a smile on her lips.

"It would be a great help," Mark echoed.

"I'll also make arrangements for Mr. Wilson to be transferred up here when they are done working on him. I'll be posting a police guard twenty-four hours a day."

"Be sure to handpick your people," Mark said.

"I always do when it's one of my cases."

As soon as Geanie and Lorraine left, Mark went and sat next to Cindy. She reached out and grabbed his hand.

"What if he knows about Jeremiah?" she whispered.

"I don't think he has the kind of connections to know anything," Mark said. "However, if he's been observing us for a while, he might be able to reasonably guess that our favorite rabbi is living out his second life."

"Mark, I'm scared," she whispered.

"I know. Me, too," he admitted.

~

Jeremiah had thoroughly tested the ropes that held him tied to the chair. He didn't want to undo them just yet because he still didn't know where Cindy was and if Matthews was in a position to easily make good on his threat to have her killed. He had determined that it would take him less than twenty seconds to slip the ropes when he was ready.

The door opened and he tensed, waiting for another opportunity to rattle Matthews. He was disappointed and more than a little wary when Sadie stepped through the door instead.

She had her hair up in pigtails and her hands were clasped behind her back. The way she moved toward him reminded him of a five-year-old excited to tell their parent something.

"You upset Father," she said in a chiding voice.

"Sorry to hear it," he said, watching her closely. She was unpredictable and that made her especially dangerous.

"It was naughty of you. You're a very naughty boy indeed."

"Am I?" he said, keeping his voice neutral as he watched her sauntering closer and closer.

"You shouldn't have caused father so much trouble."

She stopped in front of him. "You know what happens to naughty boys?"

"What?"

"They get sent to bed without any supper."

Quick as a cat, Sadie whipped a needle out from behind her back.

Jeremiah stood partially up, the chair still tied to him. He spun and knocked it into her. She fell but managed to keep hold of the needle. He twisted back around, the chair hitting her in the forehead.

The skin split open, and blood began flowing down her face. She let out a piercing scream.

Jeremiah's fingers worked the ropes. Sadie slammed her forehead into his knee, shoving it backward and into the chair. Pain knifed through him as his leg gave way and he toppled over sideways, landing hard on his shoulder. Sadie scrabbled forward and jabbed the needle into his arm.

"Time for you to go nighty night."

He tried to push up off the ground, but it was no use. Whatever had been in that needle was working fast.

"Tell your father to go to-"

He didn't get to finish his sentence as his temple slammed into the cold concrete.

~

Four hours later Cindy had been discharged and she and Mark were standing in Gerald's newest hospital room. The man looked terrible with gauze covering half his head. The doctor had said he was lucky. Whatever he'd been struck with had only glanced off his skull. He'd needed twenty stitches, but he would be alright.

He had finally come out from under the sedation, but the nurses warned that he probably would only be conscious for a couple of minutes before going back to sleep. He had been trying to talk to them for the last five minutes with limited success.

It was frustrating, but Cindy was forcing herself to try and stay calm. Getting agitated with him didn't do any of them any good.

"It's okay. You're safe now. You can rest up and we can talk tomorrow," she told him with what she hoped was a reassuring smile.

"No," he whispered.

"No?" she asked surprised.

"Have to tell before he kills me," Gerald said doggedly, struggling to get each word out.

"Okay, tell us," Cindy said.

"Green Pastures was first, not last," Gerald said, clearly struggling to speak.

"What do you mean it wasn't last?" Mark asked.

"Seven other cults…Matthews…more kidnapped children."

"You mean he moved to other locations and created new cults, or an extension of his old one, and started up in the kidnapping business at every one?" Cindy asked, wanting to make sure she was understanding him correctly.

"Yes. None as…successful. But some still missing."

Gerald's eyes were closing, and the last few words came out much slower.

"Where?" Mark asked.

"Out…side…Knoxville."

"Tennessee?" Mark asked.

Gerald was unconscious.

~

"I'm sorry, but how does that help us?" Traci asked later when Cindy and Mark told the others what they'd learned from Gerald.

"Everything we can learn about him helps us," Joseph said grimly. "You always want as much information about an enemy…or a business rival…as possible," he said.

"Well, we know almost nothing about him so we're doing really well," Cindy said, struggling to hold in the sarcasm and failing.

"Actually, your friend Jordan reached out. He thinks he might have a lead on him."

"What?" Mark asked, sounding as desperate as she felt.

"He noticed that there's a new Krewe that's scheduled to hold a parade and a ball this weekend."

"What makes him think it's connected to Matthews?"

"It's called Unmasking King Krewe. Jordan figured that given the skin masks, that might mean something."

"Sadie called him the King of New Orleans," Mark said thoughtfully.

"It says that the guest of honor is a rabbi. Given that mardi gras itself is tied to Catholic culture I'd say that's a little unusual and specific," Joseph said.

"He's not even trying to hide," Cindy said. She could feel her blood running cold. She tried to comfort herself, though, with the thought that if Jeremiah was the guest of honor hopefully that meant he was still alive.

"I say we show up to the parade on Saturday morning and see what we see," Joseph said.

"What about the ball?" Traci asked.

"Apparently there is a ball, but the group's website says it's by invitation only and there is no contact information or anything else," Joseph said.

There was a sudden knock on the door, and they all froze. The knock came again.

"This is the manager," a man's voice said through the door.

Joseph stood up and walked to the door.

"Careful," Mark warned.

Joseph looked through the peephole then slowly opened the door. Cindy could see past him into the hall. She recognized the man from when they'd checked in.

The manager grimaced. "I'm sorry to disturb you. I'm not sure if I should be calling the police straight away, but this was left for you with the doorman downstairs. I intercepted it on its way up here." He held out a box.

"Thank you," Joseph said, gingerly taking the package. "We'll call the detectives we've been working with."

"Stanley, our doorman, has been working for us for thirty years. I trust him completely. He told me a bike messenger dropped it off. He didn't notice what the messenger looked like. He was just so surprised that the package was being left with him."

"Understood," Joseph said.

Mark was on the phone with Detective Lorraine before Joseph could even finish with the manager and close the door.

"Are we going to wait?" Geanie asked. "Or open it now and get it over with?"

"Open it," Cindy whispered, walking over to Joseph.

"Are you sure?" he asked.

"Yes."

He took the lid off the gold and purple box. Inside was an all-too-familiar sight. The only difference was that this mask was smaller, almost child-sized.

"What does it say?" Cindy asked, staring in horror at the death mask. She could tell there was writing on the inside, but she couldn't get her eyes to focus on it.

Mark picked it up gingerly with a pair of tweezers and turned the mask so he could read it.

"It's an invitation to a Carnival ball," Mark said, his voice a hoarse whisper. "Which will end with…"

He drifted off as though he couldn't bring himself to say it.

"With what?" Cindy demanded.

He looked up at her, shock and fear on his face.

"A final unmasking."

20

Cindy felt herself falling. Arms were around her, catching her, but they weren't his. Jeremiah wasn't there she reminded herself. He had been taken by that monster. And the final unmasking had to be a reference to—

"Jeremiah," Geanie whispered. "He plans to kill Jeremiah."

"No, he plans to kill all of us," Joseph said.

"What if he's already killed Jeremiah and this is just a trap for the rest of us?" Traci asked. "What then?"

"We could run," Geanie said.

"He knows where we live," Mark countered.

"We can disappear. We have the means to do so," Joseph said quietly.

"I don't know about the rest of you, but I don't want to spend the rest of my life looking over my shoulder for this guy. I've seen hunted people. That's no way to live," Mark said.

Someone had maneuvered Cindy into a chair. She had only barely heard what the others were saying, but she'd gotten the gist of it.

"He has to be stopped," she said, her voice sounding alien to her.

"Cindy, did you say something?" Joseph asked.

"He's just going to go on killing and killing and destroying lives. He has to be stopped. We have to stop him."

"The police-" Traci started to say.

"Can't catch him or they would have any time in the last three decades," Cindy said.

She could see Traci glance defensively at Mark.

"She's right," the detective said softly. "As much as I hate to admit it, this doesn't seem to be a job for the police."

"There's no reason why we can't bring them into it, though," Joseph said.

"Unless they're part of his little cabal, already in his pocket," Mark said bitterly.

"Detective Lewis doesn't strike me as the type who would be in anyone's pocket," Geanie said.

"What about her partner?" Joseph asked.

Mark shook his head. "He's the wild card. There's something about him that's…"

"Creepy?" Cindy suggested.

"I was thinking more of a deep thinker."

"That doesn't make him a villain," Geanie said.

"Of course not. It's just that I can't read him at all," Mark said. He turned to Cindy. "Did Jeremiah give you any indication if he thought we could trust the man?"

It was telling that Mark thought that Jeremiah might have picked up on something that he didn't. Truth was, Jeremiah likely had, but whatever it was, he hadn't shared it with her.

"No."

"Right back to where we started," Mark muttered.

"Maybe we can invite Lewis and tell her to leave her partner out of it."

Mark shook his head. "Unless she suspects something about him herself she won't want to do that. After all, they've got history and she's got a heck of a lot more reason to trust him than us."

"Then I say we invite them both in, if they're willing to do what it takes," Cindy said. "Jordan, too."

"How did your conversation with him go?" Mark asked with a frown. "I never thought to ask with all that's happened."

"Well. He's nervous, scared, but I think he'll do what he can to help."

"Let's hope it's not too little, too late," Joseph said.

~

Looking around the room, Mark could see the defeat in everyone's faces. He could hear it in their voices, too. In their hearts they already believed they had lost Jeremiah. Which was ridiculous. The man had more lives than a cat and if any of them could survive whatever was happening, it was him.

"If Jeremiah doesn't kill Matthews and stroll in here all nonchalant in the next day, then we have to be prepared to go to the ball and give him the diversion he needs to end Matthews," Mark said.

That got everyone's attention.

"You think Jeremiah can escape?" Joseph asked.

"I think he's already planning his way out of wherever he is. Still, in case he could use some assistance, we should come up with our own plan."

"How? Matthews has got a small army at his disposal," Traci said.

"You know what? I think that's what he wants us to believe. I don't think it's the actual truth. Sure, he knows this town and he knows some of the people in it. Some of them might be helping him without really realizing what they're doing. As far as actual bad guys, though, I think we're just dealing with the three of them. Matthews and his two twisted protégés," Mark said.

"You don't think he has this town wired?" Geanie asked.

"No, I think he has us wired. He's had us chasing our own tails since the minute we got here. The man's playing games and it's time we changed the rules on him," Mark said.

"How can you be certain?" Joseph asked.

"I can't, but look, if he had more than a couple of people working for him then he wouldn't have had to send the same guy to get Gerald and to come attack you here at the hotel a few minutes later. He would have sent a person, or multiple people, to each. The guy in the van who led us on the wild goose chase didn't even know Matthews. He just got paid by Sadie to drive around making us crazy and distracting us long enough so the guy could do what he had to do."

"That makes sense," Joseph said. "If it's just the three of them, or even one or two more, then we can take them."

"Of course we can. He might have homefield advantage and be smart, but together we're a whole lot smarter. We don't have to play by his rules. We can make him play our game."

Mark came to a halt. They had been forgetting something. At least, he and Geanie had. With all the excitement over Gerald and Cindy at the hospital, he had totally forgotten.

"What is it, Mark?" Traci asked.

Mark looked at Geanie. “The house in the Garden District, where the van driver was supposed to lead us. We never went there or checked up on it.”

Geanie glanced at her phone. “It was several hours ago at this point that we were supposed to arrive.”

“What are you talking about?” Cindy asked.

“Yeah, fill the rest of us in,” Joseph added.

“The van driver who led us on the wild goose chase told us that he was going to get paid the second half of his money when we got to a certain house in the Garden District. A woman, who sounded like Sadie, told him it was part of a road rally.”

“What house in the Garden District?” Cindy asked while Joseph turned toward his computer.

Mark gave them the address. Joseph pulled it up on a map on the computer and Cindy moved over to take a look at it. Once she saw it, she scowled.

“What is it?” Mark asked her.

“That’s close to where Jeremiah and I were attacked. Danny, or whoever he is, led us straight there.”

“It would make sense that this is where Danny was leading you and Jeremiah to the same place that the van driver was leading Mark and Geanie.”

“To what end?” Geanie asked. “It couldn’t have been to capture all of us. After all, they only took Jeremiah and left Cindy.”

“What if they just wanted Jeremiah but didn’t know if he would be in the group that stayed here or the group that went to the hospital to try and save Gerald?” Joseph theorized.

“So, to be on the safe side, they had two different ways to get him to follow and fall into their trap,” Mark said.

"But why was he after him?" Traci asked.

"Because he's the most dangerous," Joseph suggested.

"Or because he was there when Not Paul died," Mark said.

"Because he's the only one who has an assumed identity," Cindy said quietly.

That we know of, Mark thought with a glance at Geanie.

Geanie was busy staring at her husband with narrowed eyes. Mark and she still hadn't gotten to finish that conversation about their suspicions concerning Joseph.

"Do you think we should go take a look at that house?" Joseph asked.

Mark shook his head slowly. "I don't think Matthews is there waiting around to be captured. And I think whatever trap he's set was already sprung. At this point it's probably nothing more than an empty building and a waste of our time."

"How can we be sure?" Traci asked.

"I don't want to risk one or all of us going there," Mark said.

"Send Lorraine and her partner. I know that we don't entirely trust them in this, but better to send police who will be missed if they disappear," Joseph said.

"I can't think of a better plan," Mark admitted.

He got out his phone and quickly texted Lorraine their suspicions. Within moments she responded that she would personally follow up on the house angle. He also told her about the mask that was child-sized. She promised to send someone for it.

"Well, we'll see what happens," Mark said as he pocketed his phone. "They've got their next move and it's time for us to think about ours. The important thing at this point is that we need to stop letting Matthews dictate our actions to us."

"So, we're not going to the ball?" Traci asked with a frown.

"Oh no, we're going to the ball. We don't want to risk him hurting Jeremiah if we don't show, but we're not going in through the front door. At least, not all of us," Mark said.

"What about those other cults?" Geanie asked with a frown. "There were other kidnapped kids."

"Those cults never got as fully established as the one in southern California," Mark pointed out. "And we don't know what happened to the members or the handful of kids that were kidnapped. It's possible he murdered all of them like he murdered the people at Green Pastures. Someday they'll find more mass graves."

"Such a monster," Traci muttered, wrapping her arms around herself.

"That's why he must be stopped," Cindy said, her voice wooden. "He's just going to keep on killing and destroying until he's the one in a grave."

Mark grimaced. Cindy didn't usually go so dark, but he could understand why. These were not normal circumstances, even for them. With Jeremiah in the hands of that madman he was surprised she was coherent at all.

"So, what do we do?" Geanie asked.

"First, we need to get supplies."

"What kind of supplies?" Joseph asked.

"Weapons, some tech toys, communication devices, and clothes."

"Clothes?" Geanie asked incredulously.

Mark smiled. "You can't expect to go to the ball dressed in rags."

~

Cindy felt sick to the bottom of her soul. It would be the ultimate irony, the worst twist of fate, to lose Jeremiah now. It would make it even harder to lose him because of a psychopath like Matthews. Rage was simmering in her and for the first time in her life she felt that she might be truly capable of killing another human being.

Jeremiah had taught her how. Had taught all of them over the last few weeks. Deep down she had never thought she'd have to use those skills, at least, not the deadly ones. In her heart of hearts she had always assumed he'd be there to do what needed to be done.

But he wasn't and she was staring down her own soul, wondering if she had it in her. She wasn't sure which scared her more, the thought that she might have what it took to kill Matthews or the fear that she might not be able to stop herself if given the opportunity.

She shivered, feeling absolutely sick.

Traci, too, was looking green around the gills. The other woman got up abruptly and headed for the bathroom. Moments later Cindy could hear her retching. She sympathized. She wanted to vomit herself. She remained in her seat, though, trying not to listen to Traci. She tried to focus on the plan that Mark was laying out, but it was hard.

At one point she nodded, agreeing to contact Jordan and see if he would help them on the actual night. It was more than he had agreed to sign up for, but even he had to see that no one was safe with Matthews around, especially if they knew her or Mark.

Why Matthews had taken a special interest in her, she still couldn't figure out. Who was to say why someone like him did anything, though.

"Cindy, you okay?"

She looked up, realizing that Joseph was speaking to her.

She nodded, not trusting her voice at that moment.

"Who is going to go in the front door?" Geanie asked.

"I will," Cindy said immediately. "He's holding my fiancée. He'll be expecting me."

"He'll be expecting all of us," Mark said.

"Yes, but the invitation, technically was sent to me."

"I'll go with her," Geanie said stoutly.

"I'm not sure-" Joseph started to say.

"It's not your decision," Geanie said pointedly, interrupting her husband.

"It's a trap."

"Of course it is. And we'll make the prettiest prey."

"All three of us," Traci said from the doorway, still looking queasy.

Mark looked like he was going to object but after a moment nodded instead.

"It makes sense. The ladies can pull focus, allowing us to slip in unnoticed and hopefully get to Jeremiah or Matthews quickly."

"Preferably both," Joseph said wryly.

"Now, I believe something was said about dresses," Cindy said.

~

“I’ve never had this little fun dress shopping,” Traci said with a sigh a couple of hours later.

“Tell me about it. We’re surrounded by all these bright, cheerful colors yet I can’t help but feel like we should be picking out funeral outfits,” Cindy said glumly.

Geanie was holding up a red dress and staring at it intently. “This is pathetic.”

“Actually, I think it’s kind of pretty,” Cindy said, looking at the frock.

“No, not the dress,” Geanie said. “This. Us. Look at us. We’re acting all defeated. That’s not us. Mark’s right, this guy has gotten in our heads and I, for one, am tired of letting him live there rent free.”

“What do you suggest?” Traci asked.

“We need to liven up this party.”

They had taken over one of the meeting rooms at the hotel. A boutique had brought in a whole bunch of dresses in their sizes for them to try on. Mark and Joseph were standing guard outside, just in case. Instead of feeling festive, it felt like they were trapped. Geanie was right. The party did need livening up.

Cindy grabbed her phone. She had a Wedding playlist on it filled with different songs she was thinking of using for the wedding or the reception. She scrolled through it until she found an 80s dance song by Men Without Hats that she loved and hit play. She cranked up the volume and immediately the music filled the space.

“Now that’s more like it!” Geanie laughed, hopping from foot to foot. She tossed the red dress aside and reached for a teal one with actual peacock feathers radiating out from the left shoulder. The right shoulder was sleeveless. She spun around with it and started singing along to the song.

A smile cracked Traci's lips and then laughter started bubbling out. She started weaving in and out around the racks of dresses, pulling some off and dancing with them for a moment before flinging them onto a pile. She finally grabbed a deep burgundy dress with a gold sash, waves of gold sequins, and a neckline that plunged all the way down to her waist.

"No one is going to be looking at anything else except your chest," Geanie crowed.

"Now, that's what I call a distraction," Cindy said, a laugh forced out of her.

She was terrified for Jeremiah still, but the feeling of being able to laugh filled her with relief. For just a moment she let herself let go of the fear and doubt. She started flipping through the dresses, looking for something perfect, worthy of Mardi Gras.

She picked up a forest green dress that was a lovely color, but it didn't feel right. She tossed it over her shoulder onto one of the tables. Then she laid her hands on a gold gown that looked like it came from an older era. It was slim with spaghetti straps and it would drape on her body. It had a bit of a train and was made of gold satin. There was a cascade of crystals down the skirt that looked like rain.

"I think I've got it," she said, turning around to show the others.

Her eyes fell on the green dress she had discarded, and she stopped and stared at it for a moment.

"I think I've got it," she whispered.

"I've got it!" she shouted a moment later.

"What? Oh, that will look stunning on you," Geanie said.

"No, not this," Cindy said. "That."

She pointed to the green dress. She had inadvertently thrown it on top of the red dress Geanie had discarded earlier. The two dresses looked stunning together, the forest green and the brilliant red shining together in perfect harmony. A kind of peace settled on her.

"What?" Traci asked, coming up beside her.

"Turns out I like traditional," Cindy said a bit breathlessly.

"What do you mean?"

"It's decided once and for all. The wedding colors are red and green."

***

Mark realized that he had relaxed slightly when music and laughter started emanating from the room where the girls were trying on dresses.

"Now that's a great sound," Joseph said with a smile.

"It is, isn't it?"

"I think laughter is one of God's greatest gifts to us."

"Maybe so," Mark mused.

His phone rang, startling him slightly. For one wild moment he hoped that it was Jeremiah calling. It turned out to be Lorraine.

"Hello?" he asked as he answered the call.

"Who in bloody hell is this guy?" Lorraine gasped, not sounding at all like the elegant, poised lady she normally presented herself as.

"What did you find?"

"Booby traps. Put two of my guys in the hospital."

"And?"

"A family of three, father, teenage son, and younger daughter. They were all dead and faceless."

"Who were they?" Mark asked as a chill went through him.

"No idea, but I'm pretty sure who has their faces. They've been dead long enough that the child-sized mask you received could be the girl's."

"Monster," Mark whispered.

"Yes, so I ask again, who is he?" Lorraine spit out.

"I've told you everything."

"That's a lie and you know it."

Mark took a deep breath. "I've told you the facts. All I haven't shared yet is sheer speculation."

"Well, you better get sharing it right now before I hand you over to the District Attorney and charge you with obstruction, aiding and abetting, reckless endangerment, and anything else I can come up with."

Lorraine wanted in. Mark nodded slowly.

"I'll tell you everything I suspect. But I need your word that you'll help me bring this guy down."

"Just try to stop me," she hissed.

21

Twenty-four hours later Cindy, Geanie, and Traci were standing outside a warehouse. The taxi that had dropped them off sped away. Cindy took a deep breath as she looked at the building.

"Are we sure we're in the right place?" Traci asked.

"This is the address," Cindy said.

Her eyes drifted upward. The buildings on either side of this one were totally dark, but the windows on the second floor of the building they were staring at were emanating a faint light.

"I guess it's time," Geanie said, her voice tight.

"Tell me again why we're wearing the dresses?" Traci asked.

They were each attired in their chosen gown. At the moment Cindy was regretting the choice of the gold gown with the train. She probably should have picked something that would be easy to run in.

Or fight in.

It was too late for that, though. They were here now. The ball was about to begin and hopefully it would be over before it truly started.

"We're wearing them just in case there's a crowd and we can slip in unnoticed," Geanie answered.

"But I thought we decided that Matthews probably doesn't have more than a couple of people working with him?"

"Just in case there's an opportunity," Geanie said.

"Besides, we might end up running and Jordan was telling me there are a lot of balls tonight so hopefully we can blend in," Cindy said.

It sounded lame to her, but she understood the theory behind it. Of course, anything that didn't involve immediately storming the building in an attempt to get Jeremiah out sounded lame to her.

"Besides, Matthews has this whole little idea of how tonight is going to go in his head, and it involves us dressing up, apparently," Cindy said.

"So, if we are seeming to go along, it lulls him into a false sense of security," Traci said, nodding at last.

"One last prayer?" Geanie asked.

The three women joined hands and prayed fervently. It was brief, but it helped calm Cindy's jittery nerves. She felt God in that moment, even in that dark place.

"There's no other ladies I'd rather face hell with than you," Geanie said, squeezing both their hands.

"Same," Traci muttered.

"I love you both," Cindy said.

They were all stalling, and they knew it. Cindy forced herself to let go of their hands. She reached up and pulled her mask down. It was gold with white feathers that spread out like angel wings. Geanie slid on her peacock inspired mask and Traci finally lowered hers which looked like a gold and burgundy cat.

"I've had attending a Carnival event on my bucket list for a while, but this isn't what I had in mind," Geanie said, her voice strained as she visibly straightened up.

"I'm not sure any of this has been on anyone's mind ever," Traci said fervently.

"Except Matthews'," Cindy said grimly. "He's been planning this for a while."

"Well, you know how good we are at spoiling people's plans," Geanie said, tossing her hair. "I think he's in for a bit of a shock."

"Amen to that," Traci said.

"At least if we can't slip in unseen we'll make a grand entrance," Cindy said, looking at the other two.

"I guess we didn't exactly pick subtle dresses," Geanie said, a smirk in her voice.

"When do you ever?" Traci asked.

"Fair. But then again, must I remind you of our Halloween party. Breathless Mahone, wasn't it?"

"I was dressing for my man," Traci said.

"Who doesn't?" Geanie asked.

Cindy thought of Jeremiah and wondered what he'd say about her dress once he saw it. It was a silly thought, really. His life was hanging in the balance. What she was wearing really didn't matter. She wasn't sure why she even cared. Yet part of her still wanted to look stunning for him even while they were rescuing him. After all, it wasn't every day she got an opportunity to be his knight in shining attire.

"Jeremiah's going to love your dress," Geanie said, as though reading her thoughts.

"Thank you," Cindy said, startled.

"You look like an angel," Traci noted.

"Warrior angel," Geanie said.

Let's just hope I can fight like one if it comes to it.

~

Mark could hear the ladies' nervous chatter in his earpiece. They were holding up better than he would have in their situation.

Especially this week, he thought to himself. Matthews has an uncanny ability to get under my skin.

He winced to himself at the irony, and the utter horrific inappropriateness, of the thought.

There was a sudden crackling in his earbud followed by a high-pitched sound followed by silence. He tapped it, fear coursing through him as he realized he could no longer hear his wife and the others.

"Well, Mark, this an interesting situation we've found ourselves in, wouldn't you agree?"

Mark froze, the blood in his veins turning to ice as he recognized Matthews' voice.

"Don't worry about not being able to answer me, I have no problem carrying this conversation."

Matthews knew that Mark didn't have a microphone, only a speaker. Which meant he knew that Mark couldn't let any of the others know what was going on.

Sweat began to bead on Mark's forehead and roll down the middle of his back. He didn't want to listen to anything the psychopath had to say and yet he knew that he couldn't stop even if shutting off the device wasn't an issue.

"So, I've been growing quite fond of you. One could say you're like the son I never…kept."

Mark ground his teeth in frustration. Tears of anger filled his eyes and he hurriedly dashed them away with a shaking hand.

"I liked Paul alright, don't get me wrong, but he lacked some imagination. Honestly, I think I would have been better suited with a son like you. You're tenacious, creative, and you have the most amazing ability to acquire… unique… friends."

Don't you hurt them, Mark was screaming to himself, wishing he could be face to face with the monster who was rambling on in his head.

"It's not that I dislike them. On the contrary, they're all interesting in their own way, but they haven't shown the promise you have. After all, the day that you tortured that real estate developer in that little interrogation cell, why, that was the day I knew that you were a far more interesting man than I'd given you credit for. I still have that video, you know. I watch it from time to time when I need a little cheering up."

Mark's heart was pounding so hard it was making his chest hurt. He had no idea how Matthews knew about that. He had to be lying about the video, though. Mark had been careful that day to turn off the camera before he attacked Frank Butler in an effort to get him to call off the assassination squad that was up at Green Pastures.

"You know what my favorite part was?" Matthews continued. "It was when you thought about killing the man."

Just ignore him, Mark told himself as he continued to move stealthily through the building, trying to get into position.

"I think you should have. After all, only a monster has children murdered."

There was a pause and then a sick, twisted laugh burst forth as Matthews clearly was enjoying himself. After all, the psychopath had himself murdered children, or, at least, had them murdered. The real Paul Dryer's body had been found in that mass grave at Green Pastures along with the bodies of other children Matthews and his followers had kidnapped. Then there was the little girl in the house in the Garden District.

Of course, the real question was how come not all of the children that Matthews had kidnapped had shared that fate. It was clear from his earlier encounter with her that Sadie was quite insane and believed that Matthews was her father. Maybe Matthews had spared the children he had broken and turned into sick perversions of himself.

Mark found himself tempted to speak out loud, to comment on what Matthews was telling him. He forced himself to remain quiet, though. He couldn't risk giving away his position in the building at this point. He just hoped that the others were already in place. By his calculations Traci and the others would be heading inside the ball in just under three minutes.

We'll see who's laughing then.

"I will admit that Joseph is more interesting than he first appeared. I'm going to have fun playing with him. My children found him skulking in the side alley."

He's just guessing, Mark told himself.

"He had a lovely set of wire cutters on him. It seems he was planning on disrupting power to the building in a little more aggressive fashion than just flipping a switch."

Mark slipped and almost fell off the catwalk. He closed his eyes as vertigo overtook him for a moment.

They have Joseph.

The thought went through his mind over and over. Things were starting to unravel.

"Such a kind face, really. It will make such an interesting mask."

Mark barely held back a scream at that point. He forced his eyes open and kept shimmying forward, trying not to rush and risk falling or giving away his position, but still going as fast as he could.

"Jordan made a rather interesting addition to your little cadre. Although he is obviously in quite over his head and already deeply regretting his life choices. Don't worry, though, I'm sure I can find a good use for his fireworks."

More tears of rage and fear squeezed through Mark's eyelids as he closed them briefly. He had Jordan, too. Everything was falling apart.

"And don't worry, Mark, I know you're not enjoying crawling around up here on the catwalk, so I'll get you down real soon."

The catwalk shook beneath his feet and he knew that someone else was up there with him. And all he could think of was that he had no way to warn the ladies that they needed to run away.

~

"Are you ready?" Cindy asked, smoothing down her dress.

"As I'll ever be," Traci muttered.

Music began wafting out from the building and the raucous nature of it did nothing to soothe her frayed nerves.

"I guess it's now or never," Geanie whispered.

Cindy stepped forward and pushed open the door. They walked inside. There were strings of green and purple lights crisscrossing the ceiling and at the corners of her vision she could see elaborate towers and arches made out of balloons of the same colors. It was hard to see much else because there was a bright spotlight that was shining partially in her eyes.

They had made it about fifteen feet into the room when the music abruptly stopped. She heard the sound of someone tapping on a microphone.

"Ladies and gentlemen, three of our guests of honor have just arrived, why don't we give them a hand?"

Applause broke out. She blinked rapidly as she struggled to focus her eyes and look around the room. What she saw sent chills down her spine.

The room was ringed with men and women in brilliantly bold outfits. Half a dozen older children moved amongst them. She stared, open mouthed. There were more than just a couple of people present. There were hundreds.

22

"We're in trouble," Traci whispered next to her.

Cindy could only nod as her eyes swept the room. Part of her wanted to scream. Another part of her wanted to run. But she stood her ground and scanned the room, searching for Matthews and Jeremiah. They had to be there somewhere. She knew it. Felt it.

"Should we run?" Traci asked.

"Where?" Cindy asked.

They were literally caught in a spotlight surrounded by hundreds of people who wanted to hurt them. She couldn't see any way they could possibly run away. Their only hope, as she saw it, was to find something to run to. If they could get to Matthews maybe they could put an end to this.

If I can find Jeremiah and free him, he can take care of Matthews, she thought.

She'd settle for finding either in the sea of masks that she saw floating in front of her.

~

Ten feet from where Mark was on the catwalk a huge spotlight had suddenly flared to life, blinding him for a few seconds even though he wasn't directly in its beam. He blinked furiously, afraid that someone or something might be sneaking up on him unnoticed.

When he was finally able to look down to the ground below and see what the spotlight was aiming at his heart began to pound. Traci, Cindy, and Geanie were trapped in it, frozen like deer in headlights.

"Run!" he screamed at them, but there was no way they could hear him over Matthews' magnified voice announcing their arrival.

In his earpiece he heard their panicked voices as they wondered what to do.

"Run!" he screamed again, even though he knew it was futile. He had never felt so helpless as he stared down at his wife and his friends surrounded by a sea of masked enemies.

He turned to head for the nearest way down to help them and froze as a figure blocked his path.

~

"What do we do?" Traci whispered.

"Scatter!" Geanie said.

She and Traci bolted in opposite directions, leaving Cindy alone in the spotlight. That was okay because that was exactly how she felt—completely alone and utterly exposed.

~

Jeremiah was struggling to gain consciousness. He kept getting snatches of light and sound, but he couldn't get his mind to focus and his eyes to stay open. Whatever they had been giving him was potent.

G-d, help me, he begged.

Jeremiah forced himself awake. He thought he heard Matthews' voice for a moment. He definitely could hear music playing below, coming up through the floor and through the blacked out windows. He immediately made short work of his restraints and stood up, being careful to do so slowly. He'd been tied to the chair for a long time and he didn't want his legs to fail him.

There was pain as the kinks in his legs worked themselves out and blood began flowing freely again. He took five slow, deep breaths, then stepped forward. His legs held for which he was grateful.

He had become increasingly aware, though, that there was something wrong with his face. It felt tight around his eyes and along the tops of his cheeks and the bridge of his nose. He raised his hand and his fingertips brushed something that felt like some sort of paint on his skin. He wasn't sure why it was there, but he didn't have time to do anything about it just yet.

He went to the door and after listening for a moment edged it open. A hallway outside was clear and he quickly turned to the left, hoping to encounter stairs that would lead him to the ground floor. He was worried for Cindy's safety, but he had to have faith that Mark had found her or she'd managed to escape the clutches of Danny or whoever else Matthews had watching her.

The hallway ended at a vast open space with a series of catwalks crisscrossing above the main floor. There was a bright spotlight shining down and he followed its beam. His heart stuttered when he saw a lady in a gold gown and feathered mask standing in it.

Cindy.

He couldn't see her face, but he had long ago committed her form to memory. He wanted to shout out, but he dared not draw attention to himself. For the moment she was safe. He needed to keep her that way.

There was a throng of masked people in evening wear surrounding Cindy. Matthews is throwing a ball, Jeremiah realized. And from the looks of things, Cindy is the guest of honor.

~

Mark's way was barred by a slender figure in a purple dress. It took a moment for him to realize it was Sadie. Something about her looked wrong, though. Her face looked puffy somehow and it was as though her skin wasn't quite attached, like it was almost hanging from her skull.

Horror flooded his soul and for a moment he felt completely dizzy. He gripped the rail next to him, squeezing it so hard that it made his hand hurt. What he was seeing was so wrong he could barely even process it. Once he knew what, who, she was wearing, his eyes refused to focus on either face.

Sadie was wearing one of the human skin masks. And it was made from her twin.

"Sadie, this isn't you," Mark said. "You don't have to do this. You don't have to do what he tells you to do. You're better than this."

"You don't know anything about me," Sadie hissed.

"I know you were the good twin," Mark said. "Your parents' favorite."

“That’s a laugh. They didn’t even know I was the one who was taken! Did you know that?” she demanded.

“That’s because you and your sister were playing at the time, you were pretending to be each other.”

“Did that a lot,” Sadie said, voice dreamy as though she was reliving the past.

“She kept on playing you for the rest of her life, because she knew that your parents loved you more.”

“Not true.”

“It is, all of it,” Mark said, desperately hoping he could reach her somehow. “She missed you and she carried that guilt around with her for her entire life. She tried to live up to being you because she felt your parents had been robbed of the twin they loved best.”

“She was a bad sister.”

“She didn’t want to be.”

“She never came looking for me.”

That caught Mark off guard. He edged slowly closer to Sadie, eyes searching to see if he could detect a weapon on her person. Although he remembered well enough that she didn’t need a weapon to be dangerous, even deadly.

“She was just a child,” he said.

“So was I! Do you know what I endured? And she got to live her nice life and not think about me.”

“She thought about you every hour of every day. She was too young to try and search for you, and when she was old enough she was convinced you were dead.”

“Was not.”

“But she didn’t know that. Even meeting Matthews’ real son, Andrew, didn’t change anything.”

Calling Not Paul by his birthname was difficult, but the impact was immediate.

"Andrew? She met Andrew?"

"Yes. As far as he knew you were dead along with all those other kids who were kidnapped."

"Stolen. That's what we were," Sadie said.

"I know. It was terrible."

Her head tilted to the side and something in her demeanor shifted. "How do you know? You weren't there."

She lunged forward, a knife seemed to materialize out of thin air in her hand. Mark dodged to the side and it only grazed his upper arm. He nearly fell over the railing, though, and he scrambled backward as he tried to regain his balance on the catwalk.

"You remember Andrew?" he asked.

"Andrew was a bad boy."

Hearing her say that in her singsong voice made the hair stand up on the back of his neck. He had no idea what the young child of a cult leader was capable of, and he didn't want to know. He just reminded himself of the man that Paul had turned out to be.

"How was he a bad boy?" he asked even though he didn't want to. He needed to keep her talking, off balance, until he could find a way to neutralize her. He realized that deep down a part of him wished he could save her, that there was still time, if not for her sake, then for her sister's. The woman who had lived such a lonely, bitter, pain-filled life deserved better than what had happened to her.

"Pulled my hair. Was mean. That's okay. Father didn't like him. He punished him a lot. More than all the others. Father told me he was going to leave Andrew behind with the others when we left."

A chill ran through Mark. Had Matthews really intended to kill his son? Had that been what inspired Andrew to run off and take on the identity of Paul?

"Matthews killed those other kids. You know that, don't you?"

"Did not."

"Yes, he did. He killed them and all the adults and buried them in a big hole in the ground."

"Didn't."

"Did."

"Father never killed anybody."

"He killed all those people and so many others, including your sister."

"Liar, liar, pants on fire."

"I'm telling the truth. He killed your sister."

"No, he didn't." Sadie said, shaking her head hard enough that her sister's skin began to slide off of her face.

"Then who killed her if not him?" Mark asked, trying not to look at the grotesque vision before him.

Sadie tossed her hair and stomped her foot. "I did."

~

Jeremiah turned back. He passed the room where he'd been held hostage and went the other way down the hallway. He was almost through the other side when he heard a muffled cry. He stopped outside the last door in the hall before the floor opened up again into more catwalks.

He pressed his ear to the door for a moment to listen. He could hear two voices and one of them sounded like Joseph's. He tried the doorknob and it turned easily. He threw the door open and dove inside, ready to attack whoever was in there with his friend.

He stopped just short of grabbing Jordan who turned out to be the other occupant of the room. Jordan cringed, but couldn't move out of the way because he was tied to a chair.

"What are you doing here?" Jeremiah asked.

'I brought the fireworks," the blogger said, nodding toward a pile of pyrotechnics on a metal table. "What happened to your face?"

Jeremiah turned to Joseph who scowled. "It looks like someone painted a mask on you," he said.

"Great," Jeremiah said with a grunt. "I'm sure it looks great."

"Actually, the opposite," Joseph said as Jeremiah started to untie him. "It looks like a bloody mess. At first I thought it was blood, that they'd already skinned you."

"No, my skin is still my own," Jeremiah said.

Having freed Joseph he turned to untie Jordan. "What is everyone doing here?" he asked.

"We're here at Matthews' invitation. He wanted us at his ball. He sent the official invitation to Cindy on another mask.

"So, he never captured Cindy?" Jeremiah asked.

"No. She was tranquilized, just like you, but they left her behind."

"They left her behind?" Jeremiah asked, warning bells going off in his head.

"Yeah. We don't know why."

~

"May I have this dance?"

Cindy turned around to see a man standing behind her. He was dressed in a simple tuxedo which managed to stand out in the colorful crowd around them. His mask, on the other hand, was incredibly elaborate and beautiful with stunning colors and wild plumes of feathers.

Before she could say anything, he took her hand in his, put his other hand on her waist, and started waltzing her across the floor. She tried to pull away, but his grip tightened.

"Come on, angel, you don't appear to have a partner. And I think you at least owe me a dance. Or perhaps I'm the one who owes you. I always get that mixed up."

They spun in and out of circles of light on the floor. After a few seconds Cindy finally got a good look into the eyes behind the mask and she saw madness lurking there.

And laughter.

She gasped as he chuckled. He leaned in and whispered into her ear.

"So nice to meet you at last."

She was dancing with Matthews.

23

Mark was having trouble grasping the fact that Sadie had killed her own twin. The fact that he'd have her do so proved just how much of a monster Matthews was.

And how much control he has over her.

In that moment Mark realized that there was no saving Sadie. All he could worry about was saving himself. He wished he had a gun more than he ever had before. Unfortunately, that had stayed behind in California.

He remembered the maneuver he'd pulled back at the hospital when he wanted Sadie to give him the gun. He just hoped it would work a second time.

He straightened up and used his diaphragm to project his deepest, sternest voice. "Young lady, hand me that knife this instant."

"Papa says I don't have to listen to anyone but him," Sadie said with a defiant shake of her head.

It had been too much to hope that the same trick would work twice. Matthews had been smart to close that loophole in Sadie's brainwashing. He'd probably heard that she gave Mark the gun at the hospital.

"Even Papa has to listen to someone," Mark said while keeping his distance from her and warily watching the knife in her hand.

"No one."

"What about his Papa?" Mark said, grasping for straws.

Sadie had been advancing on him and she stopped. “His Papa?” she asked, her voice wondering.

“Yes, Papa’s Papa. Your Grandpapa.”

He knew he was practically babbling in his effort to say something to catch her off guard.

“Do I have a Grandpapa?”

She was clearly not completely cognizant of her own age, and children the age she thought she was often weren’t good judges of adult ages. He took a gamble and smiled at her.

“Yes. Me.”

~

Jeremiah had just finished untying Jordan when he felt the ground vibrate. He dropped to one knee, reached behind him, grabbed the man coming up behind him, and tossed him forward over his shoulder.

Danny landed on his back with a grunt.

“Get out of here!” Jeremiah shouted to Joseph and Jordan. He wished he had more time to tell them to find the others or to protect Cindy, but he had to brace himself because Danny was already up, recovered, and ready to attack.

Remember, Jeremiah told himself. He doesn’t fight like a man. He fights like an animal. So, in order to win, I have to fight him like he is one.

~

Sadie stared at Mark slack-jawed for a moment and he began to hope that his little ploy had worked. Suddenly, though, her body tensed up.

"You're not my grandpapa!" she shrieked.

She lunged forward, knife swiping wildly at him. His foot slipped beneath him, and he fell which was the only thing that saved him from being stabbed in the chest.

The catwalk swayed slightly, terrifying him all the more. He didn't like the tiny space, the uncertain footing, or the immediate possibility of falling to his death.

Sadie, on the other hand, didn't seem to care or even notice that they were suspended thirty feet over a concrete floor. Maybe there was a way he could take advantage of that before she killed him.

~

Cindy struggled to break free of Matthews' grip but he just held her tighter, his left hand nearly crushing the bones in her right. His right hand was on her waist, squeezing harder and harder as he sought to keep her close, under control. All of that meant that her left hand was completely free.

They were too close together for her to have enough range of motion to effectively do much. She was, though, intensely grateful that Geanie had insisted on manicures earlier. The glint of light off her rhinestone studded nails gave inspiration.

Quick as a cat she scratched at Matthews' eyes. He let out a roar of rage and let go of her as he reached up for his face. As he did so, she stomped down hard on his insole and then turned and ran into the dancing throng.

~

Jeremiah fell hard on his back, the wind knocked out of him. Danny had driven into him like a bull and flung him all the way out of the room and back to the place where the hallway connected with the catwalk.

As he fought to draw air into his lungs he could see Mark thirty feet away, dangling from the scaffolding with one hand. Jeremiah knew the detective would never survive a fall from that height. That knowledge drove him to his knees just in time to meet Danny's oncoming charge. The other man had his head down, still moving like a bull.

Jeremiah drove the heel of his hand straight up under Danny's chin. The big man's head snapped backward painfully and his feet slid out from underneath him. Jeremiah followed through, driving his fingers into the other man's Adam's apple, dislodging it into his windpipe.

Jeremiah rose swiftly while Danny started choking to death. Normally he might have lingered a second or two to put him out of his misery, but he didn't have time. He had to get to Mark before he was killed.

~

Sadie crouched down to peer into Mark's eyes.

"What are you doing down there?" she asked with that same childlike curiosity that unnerved him. She was the one that had kicked him hard enough to send him over the edge, yet somehow she was surprised to see him dangling from the metal walkway.

"Enjoying the view. You should really see it for yourself," he said. "So many pretty costumes."

Sadie's eyes grew wide as she bent over further, clearly looking.

"They are pretty."

With his free hand Mark grabbed her hair and yanked hard. She yelped in surprise before tumbling, almost in slow motion, to the hard ground below where she lay, looking like a broken doll that had been discarded by some petulant child.

Mark felt a sob escape. Whether it was for her or for himself as he felt his grip slipping, he didn't know.

Suddenly an iron hand wrapped around his wrist, and a moment later Jeremiah was hoisting him up onto the catwalk. Mark threw his arms around the rabbi and hugged him tight.

"I thought I lost you," he said.

"You know me, I always turn up just when you need me," Jeremiah said.

Mark let go of him and stepped back.

"We need to get to the girls," he said.

Jeremiah nodded. Mark turned and led the way to an access stairway that would get them to the ground floor.

~

Cindy frantically pushed through bodies, eyes searching for anyone she knew. Matthews was chasing her. She knew it without having to look. It was as though she could feel his presence, reaching dark fingers out to her, trying to grab at her hair and feet.

He's just a man, she told herself over and over again. Having looked into his eyes and seeing pure madness there, it was hard to believe it. She was going through in her mind all the things she should have done to him instead of running. But Jeremiah had told them that running away was a valid option when fighting someone.

Suddenly her entire body came to a halt so forcefully that she almost fell over. She spun around and saw Matthews behind her, an evil smile on his face. His foot was on the train of her dress.

"Practicing for the wedding, I see. Although I hope that train is much longer, the kind that takes several small children to carry," he said.

"Get away from me!" she screamed at him.

"No. After all, we haven't finished our dance."

Cindy heard a scream and a moment later Geanie leaped at Matthews, kicking and hitting. He hoisted her up into the air and tried to throw her, but she hung on like a madwoman. She managed to kick him in the groin, and he dropped her and staggered back. His eyes were bleeding and he let out a strangled cry.

Geanie lunged forward, but a tall woman with bronze skin blocked her path.

"You mustn't hurt Father," she said.

Geanie tried to shove her to the side, but two more stepped forward.

"We will protect Father," a man in a red brocade tuxedo said, his voice monotone.

Cindy grabbed Geanie's hand and ran. They had taken a dozen steps when an explosion boomed all around them. Overhead a shower of bright purple and gold exploded.

"Jordan's fireworks!" Cindy gasped. They were beautiful and they shimmered as they rained down all around them. Some embers landed in the elaborate wig of a woman ten feet away and moments later her whole head was aflame.

It was Geanie's turn to pull her away. Together they ran for the main exit. Their way was blocked by a hundred people, some confused looking, a few scared. Many had blank expressions on their faces. The rest were staring at them with unbridled hatred.

"Oh no," she whispered as she realized they were going to have to fight their way out.

"My children! We're leaving," Matthews' voice boomed over the loudspeaker he had used earlier.

Dozens of people instantly turned away and moments later they were gone.

"Where did they go?" Cindy asked.

"Right now that doesn't matter. We have to get out of here," Geanie said, panic in her voice.

Cindy looked behind her and saw that fire was spreading throughout the building. She could hear screaming now as the first of the guests started to realize they were in danger.

"The others!" Cindy shouted.

"Will find their own way out! Don't make me carry you!" Geanie shouted.

Moments later they were outside. Smoke was beginning to billow from the building and Cindy could hear many, many sirens in the distance.

~

Through the crowd Jeremiah saw Geanie pull Cindy outside, for which he was grateful. He and Mark hurried to follow, nearly tripping over Sadie's body in the process. At least she could never hurt anyone again.

Outside, they found Geanie and Cindy. Moments later Jordan and Joseph followed them out of the building.

"Wow, I never thought it would go up quite like that," Jordan said in between coughs.

"He breathed in a lot of smoke," Joseph explained.

"I'm fine," Jordan protested.

Mark began to look around. "Where's Traci?" he asked anxiously.

"I don't know. I haven't seen her since we got here," Cindy said.

Mark turned as though to run back into the building, but Jeremiah caught him around the chest.

"She could still be in there."

"And if she is, you'll never find her before you die of smoke inhalation," Jeremiah said.

Mark continued to fight him, and Jeremiah started to think he was going to have to knock him out.

"I'm here!" Traci called, coming from the side of the building. "I found another way out."

Mark threw his arms around his wife and sobbed.

Moments later police arrived and several ambulances and firetrucks were close behind. The authorities moved them farther away from the building. They took Jordan in an ambulance despite his protests. The EMTs wanted to be on the safe side since smoke inhalation was dangerous.

Detective Moretti found them in the crowd.

"Matthews?" he asked.

"Escaped. Some of his followers, too," Cindy said.

"We've got roadblocks set up. Hopefully we'll catch him. He's got to know he can't stay in New Orleans any longer. We're on to him."

Moretti moved away to help coordinate efforts in interviewing the other party guests.

Jeremiah was reflecting on the narrow escape they'd just made. He didn't like that Matthews was on the loose, but hopefully the police net would capture him. Deep down, though, he doubted it.

24

They stood together and watched the place burn. Jeremiah had his arm wrapped around Cindy's shoulders, but despite that and the heat of the fire she felt cold deep inside.

Matthews had escaped. Detective Lewis had let them know that he'd slipped through the police roadblocks. She believed he had probably left town and Cindy was inclined to agree. After all, the cops were onto him now. He could easily move on to someplace new where he could wreak his own personal brand of terror on an unsuspecting populace.

He had told her their dance wasn't finished and she had a sick feeling inside that he'd make good on his threat. She just didn't know how to stop him at this point.

After some brief interviews the detectives sent them back to their hotel with a promise to reconnect the following afternoon. They all were happy to head back, but the sense of relief that Cindy usually felt when a mystery had been wrapped up was missing. In its place was just a bone-weary exhaustion and a sense of dread.

~

The next morning after waking up from a long sleep, Cindy went to visit Gerald in the hospital. He was looking much better, and he was sitting up and eating lunch. They chatted for a few minutes. She caught him up on all that had happened.

"Sounds like you all got very lucky," he said at last.

"I guess so."

"What's bothering you, Cindy?"

"I feel…wrong, somehow. Out of sorts. I'm used to being presented with a mystery, solving it, and moving on. Now, though…"

"There was no mystery for you to solve. There was just a madman for you to face. And, to be quite honest, you lost. Although, with a man like Matthews the fact that you survived is a victory. So, take that win for what you can."

"I know, it's just…unsettling."

"It's okay. Life isn't a series of events all wrapped up into neat little boxes with pretty bows. Life is messy and hard, and parts of it spill over into other parts of it. Some things end too soon while other things that seem like they should be over and done with drag on for what seems like forever."

"You are a very wise man," she said.

"Not as wise as I'd like. I'm here after all."

"I'm sorry," she said.

"Well, not to worry. I'm being discharged today."

"That's good news. Where are you going?" Cindy asked.

He shook his head slightly. "Far away from here…and from California. I've been in contact with my former partner. It turns out his wife died almost a year ago and he could use the company. I'm going to go stay with him."

"That sounds like a very wise idea."

"Cindy, please don't take this the wrong way, but…don't try to find me."

Cindy bit her lip. His words stung a little, but she completely understood the reason behind them.

"Okay, I won't," she said softly.

"Thank you. When I'm ready…when I have anything to tell you…I'll be in contact. Until then…"

"I understand, and it's okay," she said, reaching out to take his hand.

He shook his head. "I quit the force because I wanted a safer life. Who would have thought that a couple of interviews about a dead serial killer and a decades old cult mystery would have led me here?"

"I'm sorry I've caused you so much trouble."

"No, don't ever feel bad. It wasn't you. I led me here. My own natural stubborn curiosity. It turns out you can take the man out of the detective squad, but you can't take the detective out of the man. That shield isn't just pinned on the outside. It's on the inside as well."

She smiled at him. She was sad that she might not see him again, but glad that he was going to be safe.

"You let me know if you need anything," she said.

"I guarantee you'll hear me holler."

On an impulse she kissed him on the cheek before she turned and left the room.

~

It had taken a long time for Jeremiah to become comfortable with Mark and even longer to become semi-comfortable with Liam. It was hard to sit in a room with two detectives he'd known less than a week and go over the events of the night before with them.

For one thing, he had to return to his old habit of carefully filtering everything he said. Detectives Lewis and Moretti were both smart and observant. He couldn't afford the least little slipup in front of them. He just hoped the others managed to stick to the story as well.

As they relayed the story to the two detectives, things seemed to go well and after over an hour of discussing what had happened before they got there, the two detectives were finally ready to disclose some information about what happened after they got there.

"Two-thirds of the ball attendees had no idea why they were there. They'd gotten a party invitation and, well, Mardi Gras. They went. We're still interviewing them, but most don't even know what happened. Which is good. The city doesn't exactly want to advertise that we had a cult leader in our midst," Moretti said.

"What about the other third?" Mark asked sharply.

"That's where it gets real ugly," Lorraine said, forgoing her usually formal speech.

"How ugly?" he pushed.

"There were eleven who turned out to have been missing since they were kids."

"More kidnapping victims," Geanie said with a shudder.

"Four of them committed suicide rather than be arrested. It's a tragedy," Lorraine said, averting her head swiftly but not before Jeremiah caught the glint of tears in her eyes.

"And the others?" Geanie asked.

"In custody now. Their fingerprints came back attached to a number of unsolved cases ranging from robbery to arson to murder."

"Wonderful," Mark said sarcastically.

"My boss is happy to close that many cases in one fell swoop."

"I bet he is. What about the others who weren't kidnapping victims?"

Detective Lewis looked distinctly uncomfortable. "It appears as though they're a nascent movement."

"You mean, the first recruits in a new cult?" Joseph interrupted.

"Yes, that is what they appear to be," Lorraine said.

"Glad we nipped that in the bud," Joseph said.

"But did we? How do we know others didn't escape? They could be with him now, wherever he's gone," Geanie said anxiously.

"It's unclear if others managed to leave. From what we've been able to ascertain, this would be the first time he's tried to initiate a movement here, in his hometown," Lorraine said.

"Homegrown crazy," Mark mused.

"What about the family in the house, did you find out yet who they were?" Cindy asked.

"We're still working on that. Brad Stevenson owned the house. We think that's the man. He had two children, a boy named Drew and a girl named Donna. We're still trying to confirm identities of the victims, but that's our theory at the moment."

"Drew? Like Andrew, Matthews' biological son? Coincidence?" Mark asked.

"We don't know anything at this point. Once forensics has something concrete for us, I'll let you know," Lorraine said.

When at last they were finished, the New Orleans detectives took off, leaving the six of them finally alone.

"You know I don't think I ever want to even hear the word "Mardi Gras" again Mark groaned. "I've seen enough masks for a lifetime."

"I could use some sleep…and a vacation," Traci said.

"Um, I think we need to address the elephant in the room," Cindy said.

Everyone turned to look at her.

"Matthews is still out there with some of his cult crazies. As much as I wish it wasn't true, I don't think we've heard the last of Paul's father," Cindy said.

"Not Paul," Mark corrected absently.

"No, Paul," Geanie said firmly. "Having met his father I completely support his decision to change his name, even if he was stealing someone else's in the process."

"Agreed," Joseph said. "Whatever his initial motivations, whether he was running away or his father sent him to live with the Dryers, it's clear he wanted out and to have a new life, a better one."

"What do we do now? Go home? Just wait around for Paul's father to find us?" Cindy asked.

"Well, I'm not sure about the rest of you, but we're heading for Zone World in Florida. We could use some fun. Besides, Clarice will be arriving there in a couple of days for her last appearance in a dog show before she officially retires," Joseph said.

"You're all welcome to join us," Geanie said. "I think we might have talked about that a million years ago before we got here to New Orleans."

"I could use a vacation," Traci said, turning pleading eyes toward Mark.

He threw his hands in the air. "You'll get no argument from me."

"It's settled then," Jeremiah said, taking Cindy's hand. "We're heading to Zone World."

It wasn't an answer to Cindy's question about what they were going to do about Matthews, but no one was ready to talk about that yet, let alone try and figure out a gameplan. It made it hard when the man had the lives of a cat and was as slippery as a snake.

It was okay. They would work it out when they got home. For now, a little rest and relaxation would do all of them some good.

~

Cindy was grateful to be leaving New Orleans. They arrived at the airport half an hour early and were waiting in the terminal before they could board Joseph and Geanie's private jet.

"I'm going to use the bathroom," Traci said, getting up.

"If you wait like ten more minutes you can use the one on the plane," Geanie said.

"That's okay. It'll just take a minute and I really have to go now," Traci said.

She headed off toward the bathroom. Cindy sat there for a few seconds and then sighed. Finally, she forced herself to her feet.

"My mom always said that you should go to the bathroom when the opportunity presents itself. I think it's the only thing she said I still listen to."

"Don't worry about it," Mark said. "It's female sheep syndrome. One of you goes to the bathroom, you all go."

"Geanie?" Cindy asked.

Geanie wrinkled her nose. “Well, of course I have to go now, but I’d still rather wait for the jet bathroom.”

Cindy nodded and headed off. She reached the bathroom and saw Traci standing off to the side, her back toward her. Cindy was about to call out when she overheard Traci say something that gave her pause.

“It took some effort, but I managed to ditch it without anyone seeing.”

Cindy came to a halt, wondering who Traci could be talking to and what she had ditched.

“We’re heading to Zone World… No, don’t try to contact me there. Wait until we all get home…”

Cindy started to back away quietly. Traci’s next words made her hair stand on end.

“No, of course not. I’m a brilliant actress. Everything is going according to plan. Not one of them suspects a thing.”

Debbie Viguié is the New York Times Bestselling author of more than five dozen novels including the *Wicked* series, the *Crusade* series and the *Wolf Springs Chronicles* series co-authored with Nancy Holder. Debbie also writes thrillers including *The Psalm 23 Mysteries,* the *Kiss* trilogy, and the *Witch Hunt* trilogy. When Debbie isn't busy writing, she enjoys spending time with her husband, Scott, visiting theme parks. They live in Florida with their cats, Schrödinger and Patches.

Made in United States
North Haven, CT
28 February 2023